Beyond Missing

Raymond D. Mason

Other Books by This Author

The Long Ride Back
Return to Cutter's Creek
Ride the Hellfire Trail
Brimstone; End of the Trail
Brotherhood of the Cobra
A Walk on the Wilder Side (Dan Wilder)
Night of the Blood Red Moon
The Woman in the Field
Day of the Rawhiders
Last of the Long Riders
The Mystery of Myrtle Creek
Yellow Sky, Black Hawk
In the Chill of the Night
Aces and Eights
8 Seconds to Glory
Four Corners Woman
A Motive for Murder
Corrigan
Send in the Clones

(A Case of)
Beyond Missing

Raymond D. Mason books may be ordered through authorized booksellers associated with Mason Books or by contacting:

Raymond D. Mason
405 Corona Loop Rd.
Roseburg, OR 97470

E-mail: rmason3092@aol.com

(541) 679-0396

This is a work of fiction. All characters, names, incidents, organizations, and dialogue in this novel are either the products of the author's imagination or are used fictitiously.

Cover created by Brett Lee Mason and Raymond D. Mason

Printed in the United States of America

Raymond D. Mason

CHAPTER

1

EVERY YEAR IN AMERICA there are hundreds of children reported missing. Fortunately, the majority are simply runaways that, after a few days of going without a decent meal, return home safe and sound. Too many, however, wind up trapped in a life of drugs, theft, prostitution, or worse; the worst cases naturally being those that wind up in a city morgue somewhere. Then there are those that simply vanish and are never heard from again. The case that I was involved in concerning the disappearance of Danny Turner was one so baffling that I labeled it, "Beyond Missing."

It was the 20th of April, at exactly 9:30 in the morning when my phone rang. I knew that was the time because of the large digital clock on my somewhat cluttered desk. The woman's voice on the other end had a desperate cry for help that I picked up on the moment she spoke.

"Nick Castle, Private Investigations, Nick speaking," I said.

"Mr. Castle, my name is Norma Turner; I need your help," the woman said in a quivering voice, obviously on the verge of tears.

"How can I help you, Mrs. Turner?" I asked, trying to remember where I'd heard that name before.

"You may have seen my picture on television several months back. My five year old son, Danny, went shopping with me and vanished. It was on all the local stations, but never got national attention the way some do."

I remembered. That's why her name sounded so familiar.

"Yes, I do remember. As I recall the police simply had nothing to go on. No one saw your little boy, or at least couldn't remember seeing him. How is the case going; or is it?"

"It isn't, Mr. Castle. The police have all but given up even looking. Oh, they have his photo distributed everywhere, but so far nothing has turned up. I am at my wit's end. I want to hire your services to see if you can find out anything that might help get my son back. You were recommended to us by a friend that said she had hired you a few years ago and you are the best available."

"Well, that's nice to hear. The police haven't been able to give you any hope at all?"

"None; oh, they say they'll continue to look, but when I call I get the usual runaround saying they have nothing new to report and they'll call me when they do. I heard from a reliable source that they have one man working part-time on the case; more as fill in work than anything," Norma said, the anger, frustration, and fear registering in her voice.

"I can assure you that is precisely what is happening, Mrs. Turner. When they have no leads whatsoever to go on, they wait. You have to realize that the vast majority of cases are solved when the public sees something that they find suspicious and call it to the police's attention. When that happens, the police can then sink their teeth into the case, so to speak; but until then, it's like I said, sit and wait for that phone call. I know, I was on the force and saw it all first hand."

"That's not good enough for me, Mr. Castle. I want my son back and I want someone out there looking for him. I have retraced my footsteps that day a dozen times, but I'm not a trained professional. I ask questions, but I'm not even sure I'm asking the right ones. Will you take my case, Mr. Castle?"

I had a case that I was winding up and had actually planned to take a couple of weeks off to go on a golfing vacation, but hearing the plaintive cry in her voice changed my mind for me. I could go golfing after taking a look at the Turner case; I could give it a few days at least.

"I probably won't be able to start until day after tomorrow, but yes; I will take your case. I can't promise any real results though; you do understand that don't you?" I cautioned.

"Yes, I understand that, but at least I'll know someone is looking for Danny. Oh, thank you Mr. Castle."

"What about Mr. Turner; I notice you haven't said anything about him?"

"Mr. Turner and I have been divorced for several years."

"Oh, I see; I'm sorry."

"Yes, we haven't spoken for sometime now. Oh, Mr. Castle, how do you want me to handle the payments for your services?" she asked somewhat hesitantly.

For some reason I didn't think that Mrs. Turner had a lot of money. I seemed to recall that when I had seen her on television she lived in a lower-middle class neighborhood and had only been able to raise around five thousand dollars that she was offering as a reward. The money had been contributed by a few friends and relatives, but mostly by people that just wanted to help. I also remembered seeing the stark fear in a loving mother's eyes as she pleaded with a television camera to please send her son home to her...unharmed.

"What is the reward?" I asked.

"It's up to six thousand dollars now, but it might go higher," she said anxiously.

"That's my price, but only if I find your son. If I don't, I won't charge you a thing."

There was a slight gasp as though she caught herself before bursting into tears.

"Oh, Mr. Castle, thank you, thank you; oh, thank you so much," she said just before the tears.

After setting up an appointment for Wednesday of that week, so she could give me a recent photograph of her son and what little info they had on the case, we said goodbye and hung up. I just had a couple of things to wrap up on the case I had been working on for over a month, and should have no trouble starting on the Turner case within the next couple of days. I actually wanted to get started because the longer you wait the colder the trail gets, and it was already plenty cold, to be sure.

In case you hadn't figured it out by now, my name is Nick Castle and I'm a private eye working in San Francisco. I was a homicide detective for almost ten years with the SFPD. Becoming fed up with having to walk on tiptoes around some of the cities elected and appointed officials, I left the force to start my own business; something I have never regretted; not for a second. I like being my own boss and choosing the cases I want to work on. Independence is a wonderful thing.

CHAPTER

2

I WAS ABLE TO WRAP UP the case I had been working on the very next day after talking to Mrs. Turner. Because so much time had elapsed between his disappearance and her contacting me, I wanted to get onto the task of finding her little Danny as soon as possible.

After going to the Turner home and meeting with Mrs. Turner I took the photograph she gave me of her son and headed for the shopping center from where he had disappeared. I knew that the police had already questioned the business owners and their employees, but it was something I had to do as well. I have found that some people will talk to a private cop quicker than they will the police; but then again, for others the opposite is true.

Mrs. Turner had told me that on the day Danny disappeared she had gone to the Haynes Jewelry store to have a small diamond reseated in her wedding ring. Danny was with her when she went into the store, but after showing the ring to the clerk discovered the boy was no longer in the store. She immediately called for him and when she didn't see him, rushed outside into the mall and began to frantically search for him. She informed security that her son was lost and they had sent several guards in search of the boy. They turned up nothing. The police were then called and, due to his age, took up the search immediately.

That had all happened just over two months earlier and nothing had turned up; no one even recalled seeing the boy. Mrs. Turner had also told me something that made the entire situation even more desperate, and that was that Danny was asthmatic and on medication. He had attacks from time to time and needed an inhaler. She had just picked up a refill the day he disappeared, but feared it would be empty by now.

She had given me the name of Danny's doctor as well as the names of his school teacher, his Sunday school teacher, and his best friend's. I knew they would have no knowledge of where the boy might be, but they might be able to tell me something that he might have said to them that would help in finding him. It was a long shot, but long shots can often pay big dividends.

My partner, Michael Bishop, as well as our secretary, Myrna Thompson, had both come down with some strain of flu bug, so I was holding down the fort by myself. I realized just how spoiled I had become. Myrna was the best office manager in the world; as far as I was concerned, anyway. By the time she got back, I feared we may not even have a business.

Ever since Mike had come into the business with me, our case load had almost doubled. Mike was a good investigator that made friends easily. He was also a good family man as well as an all around good friend.

When I arrived at the shopping mall where my investigation would start, I found a parking place near one of the entrances to the mall. My first stop, naturally, would be Haynes Jewelers. I walked in and looked around at the jewelry cases as I moved towards the back of the store. There were a couple of customers inside and both clerks were busy, so I casually moseyed around the store looking at the display cases and thinking to myself how high priced everything was in here. Of course, I don't buy a lot of jewelry so it may not be any higher here than anywhere else. After about five minutes one of the clerks was free and hurried over to where I was standing.

"Are you interested in that diamond ring?" the man asked.

"Oh, no, just admiring it. Actually I'm here on official business. My name is Nick Castle and I'm a private investigator looking into the case of a missing child; Danny Turner."

"Oh, yes. I remember Mrs. Turner, and that day, very well. I was the one waiting on Mrs. Turner when she discovered the boy was missing," the clerk said seriously.

"Is that right? I take it then, that you didn't happen to see if the boy left the store with any one else...is that right?" I questioned easily.

"To be honest, Mr. Castle, I do not even recall seeing a little boy with Mrs. Turner. I was with another customer when she came in and I glanced in her direction, but I do not recall seeing a child with her even then," he said in a positive tone.

"You mean she came in alone?"

"I would have to say, that as far as my memory serves me, she was by herself. At least that's the way I remember it. The boy could have come in behind her, or perhaps ahead of her and was behind that case over there and blocked from my view. The owner, Mr. Corbin Haynes was also here and he was standing over there near the door. He does not recall seeing a little boy with Mrs. Turner, either. And he had full view of the area behind the display case that blocked my view."

"Hmm, so you must have been shocked when Mrs. Turner started calling for her son then, right?"

"Yes; Mr. Haynes and I both were surprised. Naturally we helped her search for the lad."

"Okay, thank you Mr. ...,"

"Ricketts, Steve Ricketts."

"Thank you, Mr. Ricketts. I doubt that I'll have any more questions for you, but I would like to talk to Mr. Haynes. Is he around?"

"I'm sorry, but he won't be back until next week. He had to go to Amsterdam on business."

"Okay, thanks again. I'll come back next week and see him. Here's my card in case you should think of something in the meantime," I said fishing out one of my business cards and handing it to the man, "And thanks again."

I left the jewelry store and went next door to a video arcade. If I was a five year old boy, this is the first place I would head if I got the chance. The lone clerk at the cash register looked like he had just graduated high school. He probably graduated with honors because he was reading a comic book; or perhaps he was merely looking at the pictures, it's hard to say. When I walked up in front of the cash register he looked up as if upset that I had interrupted his pursuit of knowledge.

"Yeah, you need change or something?" he asked with a frown.

"No, I need information. I'm looking for a little boy that got lost here in the mall a few months back. You didn't happen to be working the day they were searching for the little boy were you?" I asked, doubtful that this kid could remember much of anything.

"I just started last week. You want to talk to Buddha. He was working way back then."

"Way back then, huh; is Buddha around?" I asked hopefully.

The boy began to chuckle, "Is Buddha 'round. That's funny; every picture I ever saw of him he's round."

He continued to laugh at the joke he thought I'd made. Finally he got himself under enough control to answer my question.

"Buddha will relieve me at five o'clock tonight. He works the night shift."

"Okay, thanks. Don't take any wooden nickels," I said as I turned to go.

"Our machines use tokens," he replied seriously.

"Whatever," I said and headed across the way to the store with the sign that read "Comics."

If I was a five year old, this would be the second store I would head for, if given the chance. This time the clerk looked like he had something on the ball. He was a man in his mid to late thirties, neatly dressed, and reading a copy of a current Tom Clancy book. When I approached him he set the book aside and gave his full attention to me.

"Hi, help you with something today?" he asked in a friendly tone.

"I hope so. My name is Nick Castle," I said as I handed him one of my business cards. "I'm looking for anyone that might have been here the day a little five year old boy was reported as missing from the mall. It happened about two months ago. You weren't working that day by any chance, were you?" I asked.

"That would be the little Turner, boy, right?" he asked thoughtfully.

"Yes, that's right," I replied.

"Yes, as a matter of fact, I was working that day. I remember it well, seeing as how I have a little five year old myself. They never found the little guy, I take it?"

"No, the police just don't have anything to go on. Mrs. Turner has hired me to help find her son and the mall is the obvious place to start my investigation."

"Well, it's like I told the police. I saw Mrs. Turner twice. The first time, she was entering Haynes over there and the second time was when she rushed in here looking frantically for her son. As far as seeing the boy, I didn't even see him with her when she entered the jewelry store. She was alone as far as I could tell."

"What made you notice her going in the store in the first place?" I wanted to know.

"Because of the kids that had just came out of the arcade there. They're a rowdy bunch; loud, rude, and crude. I noticed a woman by herself and wanted to make sure they didn't start harassing her in any way. They'll do that; harass shoppers," he said sounding positive of what he'd seen.

"I see. Are these boys regulars here in the mall?"

"I'm afraid so. We've complained to security about it; several of us shop owners have, but nothing ever gets done about it."

"Do you know these boys names; any of them?"

"The only one I know is the one that seems to be the ring leader or instigator; I know he's the loudest of the bunch. His name is Buster; I don't know his last name. Sorry," the man said being as helpful as he could be, which I appreciated.

"Thank you Mr. Hults," I said having noticed his business license on the wall behind where he was sitting.

"You know my name?" he asked with a questioning look.

"I got it off your business license, Dan Hults," I said with a smile.

He laughed, "Oh, I thought maybe you were one of those mental telepathy detectives I've seen on television. What do you think about those people?" he then asked seriously.

"I try not to think about them, to be honest. I've seen more of them be wrong than right, I can tell you that. Well, thanks for the help. Oh, by the way, if you should remember anything else, would you please give me a call at my number on the card there? I'd sure appreciate it."

"You bet Mr. Castle. I'll do just that."

I headed on down the mall asking the same questions over and over and getting the same answers for the most part. No one actually saw Mrs. Turner with her son. That struck me as very odd. You would think that someone would remember seeing a little five year old with his mother; especially since they remembered seeing a hysterical mother looking for her son.

The more I talked to people at the mall, the more I realized I should have talked to the officers that had worked the case in the beginning. Before I wore out anymore shoe leather I figured a trip to police headquarters would be the wisest thing to do. I left the mall and headed for my car, but not before grabbing an Orange Julius and a couple of chili cheese dogs on the way. Hey, you can't expect a man to work on an empty stomach. My next stop was police headquarters.

CHAPTER

3

W HEN I ARRIVED at police headquarters I went directly to the records department. I had remained in contact with one of the clerks from my days on the force, Char Rutten. She had been with the department for over twenty years and had a photographic memory. You could rely on her memory better than you could on some of the written reports. When she saw me she started smiling.

"Nick, it's good to see you. I know you came in just to see me, didn't you?" she joked.

"Of course I did, who else? How have you been, Char?" I asked truly wanting to know.

"Not bad; not great, but not bad. How's Mike working out in the private cop business? Have you two threatened to kill each other yet?" Char said with a chuckle.

"Not yet, but hey, give us time," I said and then paused. "What do you know about the missing little five year old Turner boy case from about two months back?" I asked getting straight to the point.

"Sad case, that. John Hernandez was heading up that case. There just weren't any leads whatsoever to go on. To be honest, Nick, it almost appeared that the boy didn't actually exist. He was enrolled in kindergarten, but never actually attended any classes. The same is true with his Sunday school attendance; registered but always a no-show. John started thinking there may not even be a little Danny Turner, until he talked to a doctor that said he had treated the boy for asthma."

Char paused for a second before continuing, "Did you know that Mrs. Turner had been in a mental institution after suffering a nervous breakdown?"

The news hit me hard. I certainly hadn't heard that before and she didn't come across as a woman with any mental shortcomings.

"How long ago was that, Char; do you recall?"

"Six years ago. From what I hear, John found out that she lost another child around that time; a little boy, to be exact."

"You mean, lost, like little Danny was lost?"

"No, I mean lost, as in died. It was a swimming pool accident at the apartment complex where the Turners lived at the time. It eventually led to her breakdown and the breakup of their marriage. Mr. Turner must have gone through hell with her. He kind of went off the deep end as well; no pun intended. She would lock herself away for a week at a time and refuse to eat. I'll tell you Nick, Norma Turner was truly a mental case and may still be for all we know."

"Oh boy; I really picked a case this time. What you are telling me, Char; is that I may be looking for a child that doesn't exist. You said that a doctor had treated the boy for asthma? Did John actually talk to the doctor that treated him?"

"Yes, once; he told John that he saw the boy twice. The doctor's retired since John talked to him though and is living in a retirement village down in Mexico somewhere. John was going to contact him again, but I haven't heard whether he was able to or not."

"It sounds like I'd better have a heart to heart with John. Thanks for all the info, honey. I'll have to take you to lunch one of these days."

"Promises, promises," Char said laughingly.

"See you, sweetheart; take care," I said as I turned to go.

"You too, big boy," she replied.

I went upstairs and found John Hernandez at his desk. He was on the phone with someone, but as I neared his desk he hung up and glanced up at me. A grin came to his face as he recognized me. John and I had always gotten along good. He was a good cop; one that still had a passion for law and order.

"Well, I'll be, Nick, how are you?" he said extending his hand toward me.

We shook hands, "Fine John, and you?"

"Hey, I can't complain, besides it wouldn't do any good, anyway. What brings you uptown?"

"Danny Turner," I replied watching his face.

He half frowned and smiled at the same time, and then shook his head in the negative.

"Did Norma Turner hire you to look into her son's disappearance?" he asked seriously.

"Yep, she sure did. I hear you have some rather disturbing news about the case, is that right?"

John smiled knowingly, "You must have stopped and talked to Char, am I right?"

"Yeah, she's a regular information channel. So what is your take on this case, John?"

"To be honest, Nick, I don't think there is a child. If there is he is the best kept secret in the world. Everyone that Mrs. Turner has told me about, people that she says knows her son, have said they never seen him.

"She gave me the name of the boy's pediatrician, a Dr. Christopher Langford, I talked to him once and he looked at a file and said he'd seen the boy, but couldn't actually remember that much about him; except for what was in his medical file and that was that he had asthma. The doctor is retired and living in Mexico now. When I showed the doctor a photograph of the boy he didn't really act like he recognized him. There again, he only referred to the file on little Danny. I'm beginning to think that Danny's a figment of Mrs. Turner's imagination."

"Come on John, what about family members; wouldn't they know?" I probed.

"That's just it. The only family member on her side of the family is a sister that lives in Seattle, Washington. The two women hardly ever get together although they talk by phone from time to time. The sister's name is Kirsten Johns. She's married and has two little girls."

"What about Mr. Turner? You did talk to him didn't you?"

"Yeah, or at least I tried to. He's a drunk; a skid row drunk. I think he's lost about half his marbles somewhere along the path of destruction he's taking. I guess Char told you that they lost a little boy in a drowning accident about six years ago, didn't she?"

"Yeah, she mentioned it. She said Norma had a nervous breakdown over it. Is that when her husband hit the bottle?"

"Shortly after that, but to be honest, I think he was already a moderate drinker. The accident just pushed him over the edge. He became a mean drunk after the boy's death, from what the neighbors said. I think you're just wasting your time on this one, Nick. I wouldn't work on it too long if I was you. Oh, did Char tell you what the little boy's name was that drowned?"

"No, she didn't say," I replied warily.

"Danny," John said, watching my expression go from mere curiousness to one of total surprise. "I told you, this is a weird case and one that makes you wonder if there truly is a second little Danny Turner. Personally, I think the second little Danny is only in Mrs. Turner's mind."

"I see what you mean. This case gets more confusing by the minute. Oh, well, I'm on it now, so I'll plug along for awhile and see if anything turns up. I'll keep you posted if anything does. Thanks John," I said with a certain amount of resignation in my voice.

"Hey, I hope you turn up something. Say Nick, you might want to talk to a Dr. Saul Berg; he was Norma's doctor when she was hospitalized at the Clayton Mental Institution out on El Camino del Mar in the China Beach area. Good luck, Nick."

"Oh, one other thing, John; did you check to see if there was a birth certificate?" I asked.

John stared at me for a few seconds before answering and then shook his head no, "Mrs. Turner doesn't have one and there's none of file at the Hall of Records. She said she lost her copy."

I left headquarters with a bad taste in my mouth and it wasn't from the chili cheese dogs I had eaten earlier. I may have just signed on with a woman that was as 'Looney Tunes' as Daffy Duck.

The next place I wanted to go was the institution that had treated Mrs. Turner for her breakdown. Maybe they could shed some light on the case. The more I thought about it, the less I worried about any possible leads to finding the boy getting cold. John Hernandez may be right; there may not be any leads because there may not even be a second Danny Turner.

I made the drive out to the China Beach area and found the institute with no problem. Not having an appointment, I just hoped I would be able to talk to anyone that might be willing to discuss Norma Turner's case with me. Luck was on my side.

The woman at the front desk was a looker from the top of her head to the soles of her feet, although I never actually saw the soles of her feet. She looked up when I entered and smiled one of those toothpaste commercial smiles that seem to light up an entire room. I figured her to be in her early thirties, no more than that, and noticed right away that she was wearing a mood ring instead of a wedding band.

"Hello, my name is Nick Castle and I'm a private investigator. I don't have an appointment...," the beautiful woman cut me off in mid sentence.

"Who is it you wish to speak with, Mr. Castle?" she asked still smiling.

"Oh, ah, Dr. Saul Berg; if he's in," I said trying to match her smile. I didn't make it.

"Yes, Dr. Berg is in, but he's making his rounds right now. If you would care to wait though I'm sure he will see you in another fifteen minutes or so."

"Yes, I mean, no, I don't mind at all," I said as she kept smiling at me.

I suddenly got a funny feeling. The continuous smile she held made me start to wonder if she was a patient here that had gotten out of her room and manned the front desk without anyone knowing it. It was a little disconcerting. I returned her smile and nodded as I backed towards a chair against the wall.

"You don't remember me, do you Mr. Castle?" the woman said just as I sat down.

"Remember you; no, I don't think I do. Do I know you?" I asked studying her face more closely.

"Connie, Connie Nathan, don't you remember me. You worked on a divorce case for my sister Wanda Keyes about three years ago, remember?"

"Oh, Wanda Keyes; and you're her sister. I remember Wanda, but I'm not sure I remember meeting you. And I don't think I would forget that," I smiled a smile of relief.

"We never actually met, but we did talk on the phone several times and I did see you one day as you were just leaving Wanda's and I was just arriving. Like I said, we spoke to one another, but never actually met. It's good to finally meet you in person."

"How is Wanda getting along, anyway?" I asked.

"Fine; she remarried and is as happy as a lark," Connie replied.

Just then the door to the lobby area opened and a medium sized gentleman wearing a white smock poked his head out and looked in Connie's direction.

"Connie, when Dr. Hewitt gets here please page me. I'll be in my office."

"Oh, Dr. Berg, this gentleman would like to speak with you if you have a free moment. His name is Nick Castle and he's a private investigator," Connie explained.

"Yes, Mr. Castle, what is it you want to see me about?" the doctor asked pleasantly.

"It's about Norma Turner; I understand she was one of your patients here at the institute?" I asked as I stood up and moved towards the doctor.

"Norma, yes, I did treat her. What is the nature of your inquiry?" he asked curiously as he held out his hand.

Shaking his hand, I replied, "It's about her missing five year old son, Danny. I understand the police have already talked to you about it."

Dr. Berg took a deep breath, "Yes, they have. I spoke to a Detective Hernandez. I told him everything I could about Norma, but there is a thing known as doctor/patient privacy, you know?"

"Believe me, Doctor; I only want to know if she is delusional. I know she lost a little boy in a drowning accident that pushed her over the edge, emotionally. What I want to know is, if she is having delusional thoughts about having another little boy. To be honest, I can't even find proof that the little boy exists." I explained hastily, afraid he might cut me off at any moment.

"I can tell you this much, Mr. Castle; the boy truly does exist; if only in Norma's mind. I really don't know if she had a child after leaving here or not. I treated her for only a short time while she was here, and then I had to go to Los Angeles to our other facility down there. She was released before I returned, and, from what I was told, only after she appeared to have control of her emotions again. And, I might add, she has never been back; not even for the scheduled appointments we made for her. She hasn't kept one of them. Therefore, I don't know what has happened in her life. She may have a child or she may not have one," he then paused. "Have you checked the Hall of Records to see if there is a birth certificate on file there?"

"No, but I understand that Detective Hernandez did. He said there was no record on file and Mrs. Turner has lost her copy. Supposedly there's a Dr. Christopher Langford that treated Danny Turner for asthma, but Detective Hernandez hasn't been able to contact the doctor since he retired and moved to Mexico. Something I hope you might tell me, Doctor, is this. Is Norma Turner capable of harming a child?"

The doctor pursed his lips for a moment and then drew another deep breath as he pondered whether or not he should give me anymore information on his patient. Finally he seemed to resolve the issue he was wrestling with and spoke candidly.

"Mr. Castle, the human mind is capable of many things. It acts much like a radio receiver, able to receive thoughts, but totally unable to create them. Man has never had an original thought, but rather receives them and either accepts the thought and reacts to it, or rejects the thought and moves away from it. A person cannot control their emotions, but they can control their thinking habits which trigger emotions.

"In other words, our emotions are tied to what we are thinking. When we are having pleasurable thoughts we become happy, because our emotions are responding to what we are thinking. However, if we have distressing thoughts we can become fearful, anxious, angry, or depressed. Usually depression comes from dwelling on depressing thoughts that can be brought on by traumatic events in our life; a long illness, extreme pressure over a long period of time; or the loss or death of a loved one.

"As a person continuously lives in this state of depression they can begin to think of how people have mistreated them over the years; how they have always been "the victim," so to speak. As a result of this type of thinking they can become bitter, insolent, fearful, and angry.

"You asked me if Norma Turner is capable of harming a child and my answer to that would be, she is as capable as anyone of doing so, if, she was to dwell on the thought long enough. I personally do not think she would intentionally harm a child, but under extreme stress it is impossible to predict an unstable person's behavior. And, Mr. Castle, Norma Turner is, or at least was, an unstable person."

"I see, Dr. Berg. Oh, one last question. You said you only treated her for a short time when she first arrived here. Who took your place when you went to LA?"

"Dr. Charles Hewitt. He took over part of my case load; he and a Dr. Shuman. Shuman is no longer at the clinic, however."

Dr. Berg's words had hit me hard. This was an unusual case to say the least. Here I am supposed to try and find the child of a woman that is not one hundred percent in control of her faculties. She may or may not have a little boy that has suddenly disappeared. I could see now why the police had put her case so far back on a 'back burner' that you couldn't even see the stove. But like the old saying goes, "There's a sucker born every minute;" enter one Nick Castle.

I could see there wasn't much more to be learned from the good doctor, so I thanked him and started to leave. Looking in the direction of Connie Nathan I had a thought. I took one of my cards out as I walked over to her desk. She looked up as if waiting for me to speak.

"Ah, I thought I'd leave my card with you in case you might have to get in touch with me for some reason. That way it would save you the trouble of having to look in the yellow pages for my number."

"Oh, thank you, Mr. Castle. If I should ever need you for anything I'll be sure to give you a call."

"Yes, for anything, I mean, anytime; uh, anything or anytime," I fumbled along causing her to smile that Ultra-Bright smile again.

"Good-bye, Mr. Castle...Nick," she said cocking one eyebrow slightly higher than the other.

Was that some kind of signal? I'm good at reading body language; in this business you have to be for safety's sake; but I'm not that good at reading eyebrow language. At least not that of a beautiful woman I've just met, anyway.

I turned and walked to the door trying my best to look cool. When I reached the door I looked back in her direction. She had her head cocked to one side and watching my every move. It was working; my cool routine was finding a willing recipient. I put my hand on the horizontal door bar and pulled; I should have pushed, though. After nearly pulling my arm out of its shoulder socket and drawing a laugh out of Connie, I managed to get the door open and left, albeit somewhat red faced. Cool and I just don't seem to hit it off too well.

CHAPTER

4

THE DRIVE BACK across town was none too pleasant at all. My thoughts went from bad to worse as I thought about all the doctor had told me. What he had said about our thinking made total sense to me, however. I knew then why the Bible said that we should 'take every thought captive.' In other words, test our thoughts to see if they are from God or the enemy of our soul. Another scripture came to mind also, "As a man thinks, so is he." Think angry thoughts, you'll become angry; think jealous thoughts, you'll become jealous; think you have a little boy that is missing and you'll begin to believe it.

There was one person that I thought might be able to shed more light on the situation and that was Mr. Turner. I hadn't gotten his address from John Hernandez, if he had a permanent address, that is; but I figured that if he was anywhere in the city it would probably be San Francisco's Mission District. I knew the pastor of a rescue mission down there that seemed to know most of the derelicts by sight, if not by name. If anyone could tell me how to find Turner, Pastor Don Erwin would be the one.

I drove to the rescue mission and found a parking place directly in front. There were a half dozen men milling around outside the mission as is usually the case, but they all seemed to be fairly sober. I nodded towards them as I entered the mission, a gesture that drew a response from only one of the men. Pastor Don was sweeping the place out when I entered, but when he saw me stopped what he was doing and smiled warmly.

"Say Nick, what brings you down here?" he asked.

"Hopefully an answer to a pressing question, Don; I'm looking for a man by the name of Turner. To be honest I didn't get his first name, but he and his wife lost a little boy in a drowning accident about six years ago and both went off the deep end. He hit the bottle and she had a break down. Ring any bells?" I asked hopefully.

He nodded his head up and down, "That would be Daniel Turner; he's a mean one, Nick. I've had trouble with him right here in the mission. He's always beating some poor soul up and I fear it's just a matter of time before he kills someone. Be careful around him; don't rile him. And believe me when I say it isn't hard to do that."

"You wouldn't happen to know where I can find him, would you," I asked.

"No, but," Pastor Erwin paused as he looked towards the front door, "did you see a tall man in the seaman's cap standing outside when you came in?

"Yes, I did," I replied.

"He goes by the name of 'Sailor' and he can probably tell you where Daniel sleeps most nights. Sailor's all right, he'll help you."

Sailor was the one that had returned my nod when I entered the mission. I thanked the good pastor and went outside and talked to Sailor. He told me that if I wanted to talk to Turner he would have him at the mission the next morning at 8:00 o'clock sharp. Turner liked to come for the breakfasts, but then wouldn't eat again all day. I thanked him and slipped him a five spot without the others seeing it. Sailor smiled a smile that revealed two missing teeth and said softly, "God bless you." I left him standing in front of the mission and headed home. It was time to call it a day.

The next morning at precisely 8 o'clock I was sitting in my car outside the rescue mission. I watched as the homeless began to form a line along the side of the building in anticipation of the morning meal. There had been a push by some of the cities supervisors to force the missions to serve meals without holding a service before hand. Thank God that the obvious intrusion on freedom of religion went down to a crushing defeat.

Looking down the street I saw Sailor and a tall, thin man in his early forties walking towards the mission. Sailor was talking to the man that I assumed was Daniel Turner, but the scowl on Turner's face indicated he wasn't enjoying the conversation. I didn't know that the scowl was ever present with the man. When they got to within twenty yards or so of my car, I opened the car door and stepped out. Moving around the front of my car and stepping up onto the sidewalk, I waited for the two men to come nearer. When they were about five yards from me I spoke.

"Daniel Turner?" I asked.

Turner suddenly grabbed Sailor by the arm and shoved him in my direction as hard as he could, and then broke into a flat out run back up the street. I moved around Sailor and started chasing Turner on foot. For a man that only ate one meal a day, he could certainly run. He rounded the corner a good ten yards ahead of me and seemed to be lengthening his lead with every stride. I began to wonder if it was...not so much that he was so fast...but rather...that I was so slow.

After we had sprinted for over one hundred yards my lungs started burning like I was inhaling flames. I could hear the loose sole on one of Turner's shoes as it slapped the concrete making a totally different sound than the other shoe. I was seriously thinking of giving up the foot race when Turner looked back over his shoulder and failed to see the skateboard that had gotten away from a youngster that had taken a spill. The skateboard tripped the fleeing Turner causing him to do a header that addled him just enough to allow me to catch up.

I reached the spot where Turner lay and put my hand on his shoulder; more to keep from collapsing than to restrain him. He took it the other way, however, and simply dropped his head. When he raised it again, he had a look of defiance on his face. I couldn't help but notice the hatred in the man's eyes. His mouth was twisted into an animal type snarl and his words were as sharp as a razor as he lit into me with a string of cuss words that would embarrass a longshoreman.

I caught my breath at about the same time I lost my patience with the blue language being hurled at me and gave Turner a short right hand to the chin. He slumped forward, but I caught him to keep his head from bouncing off the sidewalk. I then slapped his face until he regained consciousness. This time the angry looks remained, but the filthy language stopped.

"Daniel Turner, I want to talk to you, that's all," I said finally getting my breathing back to normal.

"Are you a cop?" he asked belligerently

"Private; I just want to ask you a few questions about your wife, Norma," I explained.

"Ex-wife, you mean. What has she gotten herself into now?" he asked as he rubbed his chin.

"I want to know if you and Norma had a little boy by the name of Danny," I asked.

"Yeah, we had a baby boy named Danny. But she allowed him to drown in the apartment swimming pool where we lived. Why?"

This confirmed what John Hernandez had told me about the first little boy's name being Danny.

"I don't mean that little boy; did the two of you have a baby after the accident?" I asked hoping to get the man to open up.

"I didn't, I don't know about her. She may have; she went nuts, you know," Turner growled.

"She had a nervous breakdown, I know. I know the police talked to you about her reporting a missing five year old son by the name of Danny. Do you know anything at all about him?"

"Look, the only thing I know is that Norma and I had a baby named Danny that she let drown because she didn't keep an eye on him. I know from nothing about a second boy named Danny. She may have had a baby, but not by me."

I could see I had gotten about all I would from Mr. Turner. I helped him to his feet and reached into my pocket and took my wallet out. Fishing out a twenty I handed it to him. He looked at the twenty for a few seconds but didn't take it. He looked back at me as his look softened ever so slightly. Slowly he reached over and took the money and then looked at me again.

"Norma had a boy friend just before Danny drowned. She was on the phone with the guy and didn't notice that the door that led to the pool area was open. Danny slipped out and somehow fell into the pool. She found him fifteen minutes later floating face down. It was too much for both of us. I blamed her, still do for that matter, and she lost her mind. If she'd played it straight with me Danny would still be alive," Daniel Turner said in a reflective tone of voice.

"Mr. Turner, she's punished herself far more over this than you think; believe me. I don't know if she had another child or not, but if she did I want to help her find him. If it's all a figment of her imagination, I want to know that too. Thanks for talking to me," I said softly.

Turner looked at me and forced what some might call a smile. He walked away from me in the direction of a skid row bar that had just opened its doors. I suddenly felt very sorry for the man. Perhaps his drinking had been brought on by Norma's infidelity. Whatever caused the split, it was a marriage mired in tragedy.

I went back to my car and drove to the home of Norma Turner. It was time to put her on the spot, but not to the point that she might go off the deep end again. I needed answers and she was the only one that could provide them; at least I hoped she could. When I arrived at her house there was another car parked in the driveway. It was a fairly new Lincoln Continental with a license plate frame that read 'Burlingame Lincoln/Mercury' across it.

After knocking on the door a couple of times it finally opened and Norma Turner stood there in a robe, her hair tousled. When she saw me she reached up and pulled the top of her robe together, holding on as she tried to straighten herself up. She looked nervously over her shoulder as she pulled the door up tight against her back in an effort to keep me from seeing past her. Obviously she had a man in the house with her and didn't want me to know it.

"Mrs. Turner, I think we need to talk. I have some questions and you're the only one that can answer them. May I come in?" I pressed.

She looked around again and then back at me. Finally she gave in and moved to one side allowing me to enter. There was a man's sport coat lying on the couch and when she shut the door a man called out from one of the other rooms.

"Come on back in here, Norma," he called out.

"We've got company, Earl," Norma said with a certain amount of embarrassment as well as irritation in her voice.

"Oh? Anyone I know," he asked.

Within a few seconds a man in his late forties joined us in the living room. When he saw me he got a rather sheepish look on his face, thinking I was with the police. Once Norma identified me, however, his demeanor changed.

"This is the private eye I told you I had hired," she said to the man.

"Oh, you're not with the police, then, good," he said with a faint grin.

"Why is that good? You got something to hide?" I asked.

"Me? No, I don't have anything to hide. Norma and I are old friends. I just stopped by to see how she was doing," he tried to explain.

"Is that right? You wouldn't happen to know anything about her missing little boy would you?" I asked hoping to get a response of some kind. I did.

"You mean little Danny. I only know that he's lost. Cute little guy, that Danny."

"So you've seen him, then?" I pressed.

"Yeah, I've seen him. He looks just like his picture over there."

"Mrs. Turner, do you have any baby pictures of Danny. I'd like to see some; maybe a baby album or something?"

"Oh, yes, I have a baby album; but how will they help you find him now? He's five now."

"I'd just like to see how he looked when he was a baby."

"Just a minute, Mr. Castle," Norma said and left the room.

When she returned she was holding a photo album. Handing it to me she moved to the sofa and sat down. As I started to take a seat next to her is when I noticed the five one hundred dollar bills lying on the coffee table. When the man saw me looking at them he flushed.

"Oh, I owed Norma some money and I came to make a payment. That's what that is there, the payment."

"Hmm, I see."

I looked at the pictures of the little boy and figured it could be the same little five-year old whose picture she had given me earlier. It was actually hard to tell. The man moved over and sat down next to Norma. When I finished looking through the album I handed it back to her.

"What is your name," I asked, looking directly at the man.

"Cromwell, Earl Cromwell. Norma and I are old friends."

"I know, you said that. Norma, I'll be honest with you. The police doubt that you even have a five year old boy named Danny; that's why they've called off the search. Until they have more proof there will be no more looking for him. I'm sorry to say, the same goes for me. I need to talk to people that have seen him and know that he exists. Oh yes, and I have talked to Dr. Berg."

Norma looked at me with a look that would break the hardest heart in the world. Tears began to form in her eyes and she began to tremble slightly. This is not what I wanted. I certainly didn't want to cause her to have another breakdown. Cromwell put his arm around her shoulder and talked very softly to her. She managed to get herself under control and then looked back at me.

"Danny exists, Mr. Castle. He's a real little boy. I didn't make him up or imagine him. I lost one little boy and now it looks like I've lost another one. Only this time he's alive somewhere; I just know it. Please believe me. I'll prove I have a little boy, but it will take me a day or two. You'll see, Mr. Castle, my Danny is real!"

I didn't know what to say, but I knew I'd give her a couple more days to come up with the proof that there was a little boy named Danny.

"Mrs. Turner, could I have the names of some of Danny's friends. I'd like to talk to them. Maybe they can shed some light on the case. I need to know as much about his likes and dislikes as possible," I said, hiding the fact that I just wanted to see if they could confirm the boy's existence.

She cast a quick glance towards Cromwell and then back at me. I didn't like the feeling I was getting here. It appeared that she didn't want to give me any names and that was suspicious to say the least. Perhaps she couldn't give me any names.

"Names, Mrs. Turner; I need some names."

"Mr. Castle I can't give you any names because Danny doesn't have any friends to speak of," she said looking quickly between Earl and me.

"If I'm going to help you, you've got to be up front with me. Now why doesn't he have anyone that can verify he even exists; someone other than you and Mr. Cromwell here?"

"You'll know very shortly, Mr. Castle; honestly you will. Please be patient. You'll see why there's all this secrecy in a day or two."

"Okay, but something had better change soon or I'm out of here just like the police were," I said firmly.

We talked for a few more minutes, but nothing was said of any real importance.

I left Norma Turner and Earl Cromwell sitting on the sofa in total silence; a look of concern on both their faces. Something was going on here, but what? Why did she need a couple of days to prove her little boy existed? And, why hadn't she given the proof to the police? These were all questions that needed answering. I had the feeling that I had started watching a movie that is half over and didn't have a clue as to what I had missed in the first half of the film.

If there really was a little boy, why didn't anyone know about him? Why was he registered in school, but never actually attended. There had to be a logical answer and the sooner I knew what it was, the better.

As I drove back to my office I started running the timeline of the five year old through my mind. Assuming there was a five year old boy named Danny, he would have been born over a year after the death of the Turner's first child. Norma had suffered a nervous breakdown shortly after the death of her son and was institutionalized for almost a year.

Daniel Turner, Norma's husband swore he was not the father of a second baby and knew nothing about it. That was due to the fact that he had cut off all communication with his ex-wife. He hit the skids and skidded all the way to skid row. Daniel Turner tells me that Norma had a boyfriend, maybe Earl Cromwell, while she was married to him. If the boy was five years old and Norma had been institutionalized for nearly a year she would have had to have gotten pregnant and had the baby while she was in the hospital.

Suddenly a light bulb went of in my brain and I almost ran off the road. Norma has a mental collapse and goes to the hospital. While there she gets pregnant by someone, more than likely a staffer. She has the baby and gets released and no one is the wiser; no one that is, on the outside. With the exception of Norma and those at the hospital no one would know.

I pulled over to the curb and stopped. Grabbing my cell phone I called information and got the number of police headquarters. I told the switchboard operator that I wanted to talk to John Hernandez and she connected me. When John came on I asked him if he had talked to any of the hospital staff other than Dr. Saul Berg; he told me he had seen no reason to do so. Together we went over the timeline thing with Norma's pregnancy and John became almost as excited as I was when I'd had the thought.

Knowing that he had more or less been pulled off the case I told him I would continue to check things out and keep him abreast of my findings. He agreed that that would be the best thing to do. If my hunch was right there very well could be a boy and someone from the hospital could have grabbed him. The questions now were who and why would they do it?

CHAPTER

5

WHEN I ARRIVED back at my office I had a welcomed surprise waiting for me; it was Myrna Thompson, my crackerjack secretary, and Mike Bishop, my partner. Both of them had started feeling better and decided to come in for a few hours before I completely destroyed the business. Myrna had made a pot of coffee which I truly appreciated. My coffee comes out as either slightly colored water or crankcase oil and never anything in-between.

After welcoming them both back, I filled them in on the Turner case. Mike's eyes lit up like a Christmas tree as he listened to the details of the case. Mike is a bulldog when it comes to digging into the unknowns of a case. If there was anything hidden Mike would soon expose it to the light of truth. Myrna can use a computer and the internet like an auditor for the IRS can use a calculator. I knew that things would start popping.

Before the day was over I had a listing of the entire staff at the Clayton Mental Institution. Now Michael could go to work on gathering info on each one that might have had contact with Norma while she was a patient there. I also wanted to do some back ground checks on Daniel Turner and see if he had been in trouble with the law. Like I said before, I knew things would start popping now that the full crew was aboard.

By the end of the day Mike had eliminated about nine tenths of the staff workers at the hospital. It seems there was a huge turnover of personnel, some staying only six to eight months before moving on to greener pastures. Six of the staff that were working at the institution when Norma was there were either male doctors or male nurses, and that included Dr. Berg.

Knowing how hospitals operate I figured that if someone was 'playing doctor' with the female patients it would have to be someone on the night shift. The days are too busy with people delivering meals from room to room; doctors checking on their patients, family and friends visiting, and the other general hubbub that goes on routinely. Michael had flagged two men's names and said he would check out one of the names and I should check out the other.

The man Michael was checking on was a male nurse by the name of Ruben LaPorte. He had worked the night shift for eight years and had been reprimanded for pilfering some of the patients valuables; watches, small amounts of money, cigarette lighters, but, never anything of real value.

The name I was to check out was a doctor by the name of Charles Hewitt. When I saw the name I recalled that when Dr. Berg had first looked through the door of the lobby, he had asked Connie Nathan the receptionist, to page him when Dr. Hewitt arrived.

For some reason I was beginning to have a good feeling about the investigation. Maybe it was because I wanted to believe that Norma Turner was telling the truth after all. Or, maybe it was because I hate to see people taken advantage of by scavengers when they are vulnerable and helpless.

Mike and I drove out to the institution in separate cars due to the lateness of the hour; it was almost 7:00 PM by the time we left the office. Once we had talked to our staffers we would head for our respective homes. I arrived at the hospital a good ten minutes ahead of Michael due to catching a couple of stoplights on yellow and making it through before Michael. I went up and rang the bell for night service. Within thirty seconds an attendant came to the door.

"May I help you?" the man said.

"Yes, my name is Nick Castle and I am investigating a possible kidnapping. I'd like to talk to a Dr. Charles Hewitt; I understand he is working tonight," I said firmly.

The man must have thought I was with the police or perhaps an FBI agent because his eyes widened and he didn't even ask me for any identification. Opening up the door very wide he allowed me to come in and then led me to the admittance desk. I informed him that my partner would be joining us shortly and he said he would let him in as soon as he arrived.

The attendant called Dr. Hewitt to the desk and I waited patiently for the doctor to show up. After about five minutes there was a buzz at the door and the attendant then let Michael in, again without asking for identification.

Michael informed the attendant that he would like to speak with Ruben LaPorte; the attendant said he would escort Michael back to where LaPorte was working. As they were about to pass through the two large swinging doors Dr. Hewitt pushed them open and entered the small waiting area. The attendant spoke to the doctor in passing. I noticed that Michael took a good look at the doctor.

"Dr. Hewitt, my name is Nick Castle and I'm here investigating a possible kidnapping," I said wondering what kind of response I'd get from the doctor.

"Oh, a kidnapping, you say. Who is it that was kidnapped?" he asked almost too calmly.

"A five year old boy by the name of Danny Turner; his mother was a patient here under your care, I believe."

38

"No, not under my care; Norma Turner was under Dr. Berg's care," Dr. Hewitt said, again almost too calmly.

"Oh, how did you know I was talking about Norma Turner?" I asked nonchalantly.

"You said you were checking about the kidnapping of someone named Turner. I just assume you meant Norma Turner since she was a patient here."

"Yes, but she was a patient here over five years ago; why would you automatically think I meant her?" I pressed.

"Because the police questioned us about her a couple of months ago," Dr. Hewitt said, a little nervousness beginning to show in his voice and body language.

"The only one the police talked to was Dr. Berg; after all, he was Norma's attending physician. You said so yourself."

Now he was really starting to sweat. He wet his lips with the tip of his tongue and bit his lower lip. He suddenly got himself under composure and started thinking faster. His eyes widened a little as a thought came to him.

"Are you with the FBI, Mr. Castle?" he asked suspiciously.

"No," I replied calmly.

"Police, then," he pressed.

"No, I'm a private investigator," I said flatly.

He visibly relaxed. A smile tugged at his mouth.

"A private cop, huh? Mr. Castle, I'm a very busy man and I don't have time to play your game of twenty questions. So if you don't mind I'd like to get back to my work. If you want to schedule an appointment to see me, do it the proper way. Now if you'll excuse me, goodnight."

With that Dr. Hewitt turned and walked briskly down the hall towards two automatic swinging doors. I watched him until he passed through the doors and they closed behind him. Michael had been escorted by the attendant that had opened the door for us to where Ruben LaPorte worked in the laundry room. I waited by the desk until he had finished his questioning of LaPorte and we left the hospital together. When we got outside we compared notes.

"I don't think LaPorte is our man, Nick. We can cross him off our list of suspects," Michael said flatly.

"What makes you say that, Michael? Does he have an alibi?"

"You might call it that; he hit on me," Michael said deadpan.

"He what," I asked.

"He hit on me. The guys ..., you know?" Michael said holding up a limp wrist.

"Oh, he is huh. We'll cross him off the list then," I smiled. "He hit on you?"

"Yes," Michael said angrily. "What about your guy?"

"No, he didn't hit on me," I said seriously.

"I didn't mean that; what do you think about him; could he have played hanky panky with Mrs. Turner?" Michael snapped.

I couldn't help but laugh.

"Yes, he could have. He became very nervous until he found out I wasn't with the police or the FBI. Once he found out I was private, he clammed up. I think he's hiding something. He even guessed I was here about Norma Turner when all I mentioned was the little boy's name. I also caught him in a lie about being questioned by the police. Yeah, Dr. Hewitt is hiding something, but I don't know what. Not yet, anyway."

We talked for a few more minutes and then said goodnight. We got in our cars and I headed for home. I was feeling a lot better about this case now. Maybe Norma was telling the truth after all, or maybe she wasn't, but the doctor was hiding something that he didn't want anyone to know about. Whatever it was I felt sure we would get to the bottom of it before too long. I had a feeling that something was about to happen. I didn't know just how right that feeling was, though.

The next morning I had a good breakfast of half done bacon, runny eggs, burnt toast, fresh squeezed orange juice, and hot coffee. I'm not the best cook in the world, but I do squeeze a mean orange juice. After cleaning the egg stain off my tie, I took the elevator down to the condominium's underground parking facility. When the elevator door opened and I stepped out into the garage area, a pair of large, very strong hands grabbed me by the shoulders and literally picked me up off the ground and then threw me a good ten feet through the air.

I hit the wall and bounced off it like a rubber ball, falling face down. By the time I was able to scramble to my feet the same big hands grabbed me again and threw me into the side of the car that was occupying the parking space nearest the elevator. Hitting the side of the car caused the car alarm to go off which was actually a good thing for me, I hoped. This time, however, I was able to keep my feet under me long enough to realize that it wasn't just one big pair of hands that was using me as a handball, but two sets of big paws.

Both the men that were playing 'throw the PI' looked like defensive linemen for the NFL. They made me look, not to mention feel, very small; and I stand a little over six feet in my stocking feet! Suddenly, however, I grew a lot bigger; bigger in fact than the two of these monsters combined. That was because of the .45 automatic I pulled from my shoulder holster. When one of the goons knocked the gun out of my hand, however, I very quickly returned to feeling very small.

I watched helplessly as my gun skidded under the car with the blaring car alarm. The larger of the two men grabbed me and picked me up over his head. He threw me towards the elevator door. When I landed I rolled onto my back and found myself staring up at two of my neighbors. The elevator had just reached the garage level and they were in the process of exiting the elevator when I landed in front of them. They didn't stay long; just long enough to step back inside the elevator and close the door, leaving me there with the two large, mountainous sized men.

The larger man picked me up off the ground like I was a rag doll, which by this time I was beginning to feel like.

"Drop the Turner case if you know what's good for you, Copper!" he growled.

"Huh," I heard myself say.

"There ain't no little kid, so drop the Turner case. Next time we break things," the man said as he pulled my face close enough to his for me to smell garlic on his breath.

"Who eats garlic for breakfast?" I said out loud.

That was the last thing I remember before a crashing right hand sent me to La-La Land. When I awoke my head was resting in the lap of another of my neighbors, Jesse Ragan. She was holding a cold towel to my head and asking me if I was all right. I managed to let her know I was and she and another of the condo occupants helped me to my feet. That was when I noticed the blood on the towel she had been holding to my face. I knew instantly where the blood had come from by the way my nose felt.

"Are you sure you're all right, Mr. Castle?" Jesse asked with concern.

"Oh, yeah, I'll be fine once I get the merry go round to slow down so I can get off," I mumbled.

"He must be dizzy," the other woman said.

I shook my head to try and clear the cobwebs, but it didn't do a lot of good. Taking the towel from Jesse I held it to my nose and checked to see if it was still bleeding; fortunately it had stopped. I thanked the two women and, after retrieving my .45 automatic out from under the car where it had skidded, went back up to my apartment to check the damages to my face and body a little closer. I wasn't really hurt that bad; a little blood makes everything look a lot worse than it actually is; but, I did have to change shirts and put on another tie.

After freshening up, I once again attempted to get to my car. This time I made it without incident. All the way to the office, however, I thought of what the man had said, "Drop the Turner case." There was more to this case than met the eye; that was for sure. No one tells you to stop looking for a non-existent little boy; no one that is, but the person that hired you. No, someone was getting very nervous about my investigation. I suspected now that little Danny Turner did exist and whoever it was that had him didn't want me trying to find him.

When I arrived at the office I was greeted by Myrna's smiling face and a warning! She said that if I ever did any filing again while she was out of the office, she would hire a thug to break all of my fingers. It seemed that I had not filed things in their proper place. I told you she was good. The first thing Mike noticed was the redness of my nose; after all, he'd seen enough bloody noses through the years. I explained about my two visitors and Mike got a little grin on his face.

"Too close, Nick; someone's getting nervous." Michael grinned.

"I know, Mike, nervous enough to try and strong arm me into dropping the case. I guess that eliminates the idea that Danny is a figment of Norma Turner's imagination, huh!" I stated.

Mike bit his lower lip as he toyed with a thought, then looked at me with a sly look, "Nick, maybe it would be a good idea for one of us to go to Mexico; say Guadalajara, to be exact!"

My eyes widened as I questioned, "You mean you found out where the pediatrician lives?"

"Dr. Christopher Langford, that's right. He moved down there in August of this year. I was able to locate the nurse that worked for him and she told me that the good doctor sold his practice and moved into an American settlement just twenty miles out of Guadalajara. It's a swanky place called "The Voyager's Village." It takes big money to buy-in there; but the cost of living is super reasonable."

"When can you leave, Michael?" I said agreeably.

"Oh, I'd say about 11:45 in the morning; flight 701, gate C4," Michael smiled coyly.

"Go to it; as for me I think I'll have another talk with Norma. She has some pictures of a little boy that she says is Danny, but I'm wondering which Danny. I want to show a few of those pictures to Mr. Turner and see if he recognizes the little tyke. If my hunch is right, he will."

Michael looked a little confused.

"I don't think Norma has any photos of Danny number two when he was a baby. I think the pictures she showed me in the photo album were of her first son; the one that drowned; but I don't think she showed them to me because she is delusional, but rather because she doesn't have any photos of her current son."

"What in the devil are you going on about, Nick?" Michael asked bewilderedly.

"Yeah, what gives, boss," Myrna chimed in from her desk having taken in the entire conversation.

"The more I've thought about it, the more sense it makes. I think Norma had a baby all right, and it could have been by someone that works at the sanitarium. For whatever reason, and who knows what that reason might be, they didn't give her the baby after it was born. Maybe they told her the baby had died, I don't know, but she either knew it hadn't or found out later on that the baby was alive.

"Anyway, I think she took her baby back from the ones that had tried to conceal the boy from her. That's the reason the boy is registered in kindergarten, but has never attended. The same is true of the Sunday school enrollment, but again, he's a no-show."

44

"What about the pediatrician? He's supposed to have treated the boy for asthma?" Michael replied.

"Yes, but nothing was said about him being the doctor of the infant Danny. It's my bet that little Danny was at least three or four when the doctor treated him; probably more like four."

"Yeah; but, why would Mrs. Turner go to the police if she had stolen the boy back from the ones that had taken him from her in the first place? Wouldn't she be afraid that they would tell the police she had stolen the boy from them?" Myrna asked curiously.

"If they did they would be exposing themselves as being kidnappers. No, they wouldn't go to the police; in fact, they would definitely want to keep the police out of it. It's my guess, and that's all it is, that somehow Norma found out that she'd had a baby while institutionalized and found out where the boy was living, and took him. She had already lost one little boy, she would do anything to keep from losing a second child."

"It sounds plausible enough, Nick, but it's a stretch, you'll have to admit," Michael said scratching his head.

"I know; and right now I don't have a shred of evidence to back up my theory. But if Mr. Turner identifies the little boy in the photos as his deceased child, I'll start to think the theory has a strong possibility of being correct. I'll know today; but I still want you to take that trip to Mexico.

"Another thing, Michael; doesn't it seem a little odd that I'd be paid a visit by two thugs just after we talked to the staff at the institution where Norma was treated? It certainly does to me."

"Yep, like I said, someone's getting a little nervous," Michael grinned.

We discussed a few other matters of business concerning another case that we had put on hold until we heard back from our client. Michael had been doing most of the investigative work on that case and brought me up to speed in case the client called while he was, "south of the border."

After a couple cups of coffee I called Norma Turner and told her I would be out to see her again the next day. She said she had an errand to run early, but should be back home by eleven a.m. I said I would see her then and we said goodbye. Like I had explained to Mike, if my theory was right, the baby pictures of little Danny would give me the answer. This case was getting more and more interesting by the minute. I didn't know it at the time, but it was getting more and more dangerous as well.

CHAPTER
6

I **LEFT MY OFFICE at 10:00 a.m. sharp and drove** straight to Norma Turner's house, arriving there at around 10:30. I pulled into the curb and parked, noticing that neither Norma's car nor Earl Cromwell's was in the driveway. The morning fog was just beginning to burn off and it was good to see the sunlight again. San Francisco and fog go together like ham and eggs, or cream and sugar, or hot and cold; it's hard to say one without automatically thinking of the other.

As I sat there half day dreaming and half thinking about the Turner case, locked into what some might call a transcendental state of meditation, I became remotely aware of the sound of a car pulling up alongside mine. Casually glancing to my left I immediately recognized the Goliath sized man sitting in the passenger's seat of the car that had parked so close to mine that I couldn't open the door on the driver's side. It was none other than my old friends from the garage at my condominium earlier that morning.

Without hesitation I slid across the front seat of my car, or should I say I scrambled over the driver/passenger divider console and out the door on the passenger's side. Pulling my .45 while moving as fast as could, I ran around the back of my car and made for the driver's side of the Mercedes occupied by the two behemoths. I reached the driver's side of their car just as Mt. Shasta was pulling himself out, having had trouble unhooking his seatbelt. Before he had time to get fully straightened up I hit him across the back of the head as hard as I could. Once...he didn't go down; twice...still no downward movement; a third blow finally took him down.

The Mt. Whitney passenger was struggling to try and get the door on the passenger's side open, which was rather hard to do because of them pulling up so close to my car. I pointed the gun at him and yelled for him to freeze. After looking at the end of the .45 he stopped struggling and just sat and glared at me.

"You ain't gonna shoot anybody, Castle. Put the pop gun away," he growled.

"Just how sure are you that I won't blow what few brains you have clear out of your head," I said angrily.

The man thought for a moment, looked at the size of the hole in the gun barrel and sat very still. He was definitely of Italian descent and loved garlic on his food. How do I know that, because he reeked of the stuff! Either that or he had garlic scented after shave lotion that he applied liberally.

"All right, who hired you to follow me and rough me up," I demanded.

"Drop dead, Copper. Nobody hired us; we just don't want you buttin' in where you ain't welcome."

"You don't expect me to believe that cock-a-mamey story do you?"

"I don't care what you believe; we just don't want you nosing around this Turner case. There ain't no kid, so drop it."

"I'm going to find out who you work for and when I do it's going to go bad for them, as well as you and your Cyclops brother here. I've had about all I can take of you."

Just then I heard another car pulling up behind me. I turned around to see Norma Turner and Earl Cromwell pulling into the driveway. They were both staring hard at me and my two over sized uninvited companions. I could see Norma's eyes squinting as she tried to make out who was sitting in front of her house; and then suddenly they widen and she began screaming at Cromwell. Earl shoved the automatic transmission lever into reverse and gunned it, burning rubber all the way out of the driveway and into the street, nearly hitting a passing car in the process.

"Now see what you have done. You scared my friends half to death. Shame on you," I said as I watched Norma and Earl speeding off down the street.

Cocking the hammer back on my .45 I told Goliath to take his gun out of its shoulder holster very slowly and using only his thumb and forefinger. He wasn't about to try anything with a cocked .45 aimed at his head, so he did exactly as he was told. I took the gun and threw it across the street as far as I could. I reached down and took the gun out of the other man's holster as well, also giving it a heave to the other side of the street.

Still keeping a wary eye on the man in the car, I smiled widely as I dropped the gear shift of their car into Drive and stepped away from the door. The car began driving off slowly down the street with no one behind the steering wheel; although one very large man in the passenger's seat became very animated in his attempt to get the car under control. It was really quite comical to watch. It took him a good two blocks to even get the car stopped. By that time I had gotten in my car and was long gone.

I knew there was no use in trying to catch Earl and Norma, not the way he shot out of the driveway. They were probably half way to Sausalito by now. I'd have to talk to them later; if they weren't too jumpy to do so. Norma had acted like she might have recognized the two thugs. I certainly hoped she hadn't responded the way she had to my being there. But, why would she recognize the two goons?

There was beginning to be far too many unanswered questions for my liking. Either Norma was holding out on me, or I was misreading the whole crazy mixed up case. The ringing of my cell phone jarred me out of my thoughtful stupor; if you could call it that. Of course, I had always called it deep thinking. It was Michael Bishop.

"Hi Nick. I'm on my way to the airport, but I wanted to fill you in on something before I left."

"Go ahead, Mike; what've you got for me?"

"You might want to check out a guy by the name of Theodore Singleton, he goes by the name of Theo. He's a counselor tied in with Planned Parenthood. He's independent but works on a regular basis with them counseling young girls that get knocked up and go to Planned Parenthood for an abortion. It's his job to convince the young women that they're doing the right thing. He convinces them more often than not, but he does have a number that decide not to go through with the abortion.

"I ran across his name by accident and decided to run a check on the guy. It appears he might have a small skeleton or two in his closet. Several years ago he was charged with attempting to get a young, 'unwed mother-to-be' to have her baby and then sell the baby to him for $2,500, plus medical costs. After reporting the incident to authorities and then filing a complaint against Singleton, the woman completely disappeared and the case was dropped. Naturally Planned Parenthood was upset over the whole thing, but not enough to fire the guy."

"I vaguely remember reading about that; about a year and a half ago, right?" I stated somewhat curiously

"More like two years ago, Nick," Michael corrected. "Anyway, Singleton is best of friends with one Ruben LaPorte. The two of them tied together spells 'double trouble.' Like I said, Nick, you might want to check this guy out. I should be back in a couple of days and hopefully with some good news. Adios, Amigo," Michael said with a Mexican accent.

"Adios, and remember; don't drink the water," I warned.

There was a long silence and then Michael replied somberly, "Montezuma, right? I hate that guy."

After talking to Michael I altered my plans for the day. I wanted to check out this Singleton. If he was connected to Ruben LaPorte there had to be some dirt on the guy besides what Michael had just filled me in on. A quick stop at the Hall of Records should help. One of my old friends worked there and I knew he would make my job a lot easier.

The growling of my stomach told me it was almost lunch time so I decided to make a pit stop on the way to the Hall of Records. There was a small, intimate lounge on the way that I had frequented on a regular basis about seven years earlier. They had one of the best steak sandwiches San Francisco had to offer.

Fortunately I found a parking place about three spaces from the front door of 'Homer's Hideaway.' I pushed the red Naugahyde door open and stepped inside to a rush of nostalgia. For a moment it was as if I was seven years younger and walking into the lounge where the beautiful singing voice of Karen Ferris filled a packed room.

Karen and I had been an item at that time, but when she got an offer to appear as the star attraction at a dinner house in Seattle we parted company. We had corresponded for the first year she was gone, but the letters and phone calls grew further and further apart. I had often thought of her, but hadn't taken the time to contact her. I regretted it now.

I recognized the bartender and the one waitress that was working at that time of the day. They recognized me also. It had to be because of my rugged good looks and charming personality. Well, it's a thought. Anyway, when they saw me they both smiled and greeted me by name.

"Vick, how are you doing?" the waitress said with a smile.

All right, so she greeted me by the wrong name; at least she was close to getting it right.

"Say Carl, hi Debbie; it's Nick," I replied, getting their names right and correcting her at the same time.

"Oh I'm sorry, Nick," Debbie said with an embarrassed look on her face.

"Say Nick, you must have heard who's coming back to Homer's, eh?" Carl said with a wide grin.

"No, who's coming?" I wondered.

"Karen, Karen Ferris. Only it's Karen Ciccarelli now. She got married while she was up in Seattle. Some rich guy; but then with a last name like Ciccarelli he would have to be rich, right?" Carl joked.

"So Karen's coming back, huh? And she's married you say. Well, surprise, surprise. It will be good to see her again. When will she be starting?" I asked, my heart beat increasing slightly.

"Next week. When she left our business really dropped off. The evening crowd just seemed to disappear. We never found anyone that could hold an audience like Karen. But like the old song says, now, 'we're in the money,' again."

"When is her opening night? Wednesday, like before?"

"Yep; she'll be getting into town on Monday, though. She's already found her an apartment and moved most of her furniture in from what I hear. It'll be good to see her again. Just like old times," Carl beamed.

"Yeah, just like old times," I answered.

That funny feeling in the pit of my stomach was not from being hungry. Karen was coming back to San Francisco; but she was coming back with a husband. It would still be good to see her, just not the same obviously.

I ordered the steak sandwich and along with a cold beer and some French fries took care of one of the funny feelings in my stomach. The other feeling didn't go away, however. I made small talk with Debbie until the afternoon crowd hit. After polishing off my lunch I went back to my car and climbed in. I didn't drive off right away, though, but sat and thought of how it might be when I saw Karen again.

What would I say to her; to her husband? Oh, well, I'd have time to think about it before it happened. I didn't think I'd rush right down here on her opening night. I'd let her get settled in first. But if Carl or Debbie told Karen they had seen me, she might wonder why I wasn't here to welcome her back. This was going to be awkward no matter what I did.

Finally I drove on to the Hall of Records and gradually got my mind off Karen and back onto the business at hand. Chorge Kaku was sitting at his desk when I entered, but when he saw me he got up and moved to the counter.

"Nicky, how are you doing?" he said with that great smile of his.

"Good, Chorge, how are you? Still shooting under par?" I asked as we shook hands.

"Yeah, right; no, I'm still playing just under bogey golf. But, hey, it's just a game, right?" Chorge laughed.

"That's what I keep telling myself."

We made small talk for a few minutes and then I told him who I wanted to check on. When he heard the name Theodore Singleton he looked funny.

"You're the second one in two days that was looking for information on him. What did he do, rob a bank, or a place where the big money is, like a gas station?"

"Someone else wanted to know about Singleton," I asked curiously?

"Yeah, two guys that look like they should be wearing football uniforms. These boys were big, and rather rude."

"I know; I met both those mountains. I call them Mt. Shasta and Mt. Whitney," I said rubbing my jaw.

Chorge looked around as if checking to see if anyone was listening, which they weren't seeing as how it was just the two of us in the room. Once satisfied he couldn't be overheard he spoke in a quiet voice.

"I didn't give them all the info I had on the guy. He's a two file folder guy; they only got the older stuff. I'll give both folders to you, though. To be honest Nick, I think these two just wanted his latest address. At least that seemed to be what they were most interested in."

"Hmm, that's interesting. Could I see what you have on him, Chorge? Also I want to check on a Ruben LaPorte; where would I find his file?"

"I'll get it for you. He's another one that has had some action lately. About two weeks ago John Hernandez was in checking on him. You might want to talk to John," Chorge offered, knowing that John and I were old friends. "Say, I heard about Michael Bishop taking early retirement and going into business with you; that's great."

"Yeah, he's a real asset. He's headed 'South of the Border' right now. Checking on a guy that retired in Mexico," I replied.

"That's the way to go. You're retirement dollar goes a lot farther down there, that's for sure. Well, let me get the information you want. Be right back."

Chorge disappeared down one of the long aisles of file cabinets and I moved over to a chair and picked up a Sports Illustrated magazine off the end table next to it. After about five minutes Chorge reappeared with three rather large folders in his hands. I went through the files on the two men and found some very interesting information on both.

Singleton and LaPorte had worked together at the same small hospital in the LA area for a time. It was named La Combs Medical Center. The hospital specialized in treating unwed, unemployed pregnant women. Both men had lost their jobs when the hospital was closed due to a scandal involving the selling of babies. Neither LaPorte nor Singleton was charged, but they were both working there when the story broke. I couldn't help but wonder, though, if they weren't directly involved in the racket. If not, that could be where they got the idea to start up their own 'Babies R Us" business.

LaPorte had a list of priors that would make Al Capone jealous. There were fifteen assault and battery charges against the man, as well as half-a-dozen busts for spousal abuse that had all been dropped when the two different wives involved refused to press charges. That appears to be the case much too often. I guess love, or perhaps it's a case of fear, will do that to people. He must have been a switch hitter, though, because Michael had said that LaPorte had hit on him. Of course, that could have been just a cover.

After going over everything there was on the two men and taking notes of things I felt would be helpful, I thanked Chorge and left. My next stop was the address of Ruben LaPorte. It wasn't that I wanted to talk to him as much as just see where he lived. I don't really know why I decided to drive to his residence; it was almost as if compelled to do so.

When I arrived at LaPorte's address, which I had obtained from his file, I knew instantly that something was amiss. It could have been the fact that the front door was open; not wide, just a crack. I hadn't intended to make my presence known, but after watching the house for several minutes decided it might be a good idea to at least look inside.

I walked up the front porch steps quietly and peered through the crack in the doorway. When I didn't see anyone, I slowly pushed the door open and checked out the living room; nothing out of the ordinary, if you call a messy living room ordinary. I called out LaPorte's name, but there was no answer. Slowly and cautiously I moved inside the house, calling out the man's name again. Still no response.

There was no one in the kitchen that was just off the small dining area that was adjacent to the living room. Someone had been here though, and recently. There was a full pot of coffee on the Mr. Coffee burner and two pieces of toast sticking up out of the toaster. The coffee 'ready' light was off, so I knew the pot had been brewed earlier. When I felt the toast I found it was cold, also. I knew then that something was definitely wrong.

Leaving the kitchen I moved down the hallway towards the master bedroom which appeared to be at the end of the hall. The sound of running water caught my attention as I passed one of the doors that obviously was the bathroom. I knew it was the bathroom because of the sound of running water and the fact that the carpet in the hallway was soaking wet.

I pushed the bathroom door open and looked in. Water was spilling over the bathtub and onto the tile floor. What I noticed first, however, was the body of a man floating face down in the tub of water. It was Ruben LaPorte; or should I say, the late Ruben LaPorte.

Before leaving the bathroom I turned the water off using the main valves rather than the ones on the tub itself. No point in flooding the whole house. Once that was done I grabbed my cell phone and dialed 911. I gave the dispatcher the details and told her I'd wait for police to arrive. I figured it would take them about five to ten minutes to arrive and if I hurried that should be plenty of time to check around for anything of interest in my case.

Careful not to leave any fingerprints, or destroy any that the police might be interested in, I went through the drawers in the master bedroom, but found nothing there. I looked in the large clothes closet and found nothing but the usual things, until I started to close the door. That's when I noticed a metal box behind the shoe rack that was filed with shoes. Wasting no time, I grabbed the box and opened it.

"Jackpot," I said a loud.

The box contained photographs of babies. Most of them were newborns, but there were a couple that were older; perhaps around two or three years of age. Why would a man have pictures of twenty or so different babies, and babies of different nationalities, I might add, hid away in a clothes closet? Duh, I wonder.

I heard the sound of a siren in the distance and knew I'd have to hurry if I was going to get this out of the house before the first car arrived. Running down the hallway I headed for the door with the box under my arm. Just as I started out the door, however, the first patrol car pulled up in front of the house. Turning around I ran into the kitchen and out the back door. The back yard was very small and the five foot high fence across the back was my best bet in hiding the box.

I looked over the fence and saw just what I needed. It was a huge dumpster on the opposite side of the alleyway that separated the homes. The house behind LaPorte's was being remodeled and the dumpster had been left there for the old building material. I didn't see anyone working on the house at the time, so I threw the metal box high enough and far enough to land it in the dumpster. Once that was accomplished I hurried back through the kitchen in order to meet the police officers that had just arrived.

As I walked back through the kitchen and into the small dining area the two uniformed cops greeted me with guns drawn. I recognized one of the cops from my days on the force. It was Gary Hammons. Luckily, Gary recognized me too.

"Say Gary, you guys got here quick," I complimented.

"Nick, what's going on here?"

"I stopped by to ask this guy a few questions in regards to a case I'm working on and I found him swimming face down in his bathtub; fully clothed and the water still running. Now, I ask you; who takes a bath that way? I figured I'd better call you boys right away."

I led the two patrolmen down the hallway to the bathroom. When Gary looked in and noticed the water was not running he cast a quick glance at me.

"Thought you said the water was running, Nick?"

"It was, but I turned it off. No point in wasting good water," I said and paused intentionally, "Don't worry, Gary, I used the main water valves over there," I said pointing to the two valves that fed the lines to the tub/shower.

Gary grinned as if to say, "I thought I had you, but you got away."

I answered all the questions that the officers asked me and shortly two more police cars arrived; one patrol car and one unmarked sedan. The investigators in the unmarked car took charge of the murder scene and asked me the same questions that Gary had asked me earlier. They were satisfied with my answers and said that I was free to go, but would I come by the office the next day and fill out a formal statement. I assured them I would and left.

One thing was unmistakably clear; LaPorte had been involved in something big enough to get him killed. Whatever it was must be very lucrative, highly illegal, or both. I'd hoped to get some information from LaPorte, but other than the box of baby pictures I'd have to get my questions answered by someone else. I figured that my two Goliath sized goons were in this up to their 'size twenty-two' necks.

I made a half circle around the block and drove down the alleyway where the huge dumpster was located that I had tossed the box of baby pictures into. I had no trouble retrieving the box, and I might add, without being seen by anyone. My next stop was the home of one Theodore

Singleton. I just hoped he hadn't decided to go for a swim in his bathtub as well.

CHAPTER

7

SOMETIMES LIFE seems to come at you so fast you don't know whether you should jump or duck. That's the way I was beginning to feel on this Turner case. Every time I thought I might be getting a handle on things, things changed and I was left holding a handle with nothing attached to it.

Theodore Singleton lived in an upscale neighborhood where yards are maintained by gardeners with Asian or Mexican names instead of the homeowners. I drove up the half circle driveway and parked in front of the colonial style house. The house wasn't overly large, but large enough that the two pillars on either side of the doorway didn't look out of place. I especially liked the little black jockey standing off to one side and holding a brass ring where you could tie your horse. Obviously Singleton wasn't afraid of the NAACP.

I walked up to the front door and rang the bell. The chimes sounded inside and made a hauntingly melodic sound. I tried to think what the tune was that played but wasn't able to 'name that tune.' Shortly the door opened and I stood staring at a French maid in a black and white, ruffled, short skirted uniform.

I told the young woman my name and handed her my card. I asked if Mr. Singleton was at home and she informed me that he was, but had friends visiting from out of town. I told her it was important that I speak to him and she opened the door wide enough for me to enter. I followed her inside.

The home's décor provided more evidence that Theodore Singleton had money as well as good taste. As I attempted to put a face on the man that lived here, I envisioned him coming down the staircase wearing a red or blue smoking jacket and smoking a cigarette in a long cigarette holder. The maid showed me into the library and with a slight French accent told me that she would inform Mr. Singleton of my presence.

I looked at the two walls of books and noticed several Charles Dickens' novels, along with Ernest Hemmingway, Robert Louis Stevenson, John Steinbeck, Truman Capote, and Gore Vidal. I also noticed an Erskine Caldwell and Harold Robbins. It appeared that Mr. Singleton had a wide range of literary preferences.

In a couple of minutes the library door opened and Theodore Singleton entered. He was a small man nattily dressed, wearing a silk robe over his suit pants, white shirt, and black ascot. He held a cigarette in a long cigarette holder and exhaled a plume of pale gray smoke upward as he entered the room. His hair was dyed black and was neatly combed and he sported a thin moustache, reminiscent of Clark Gable. I had missed on the smoking jacket, but not by much.

"Yes, Mr. Castle, how may I be of service to you?" Singleton said in a very proper voice.

"I want to talk to you about a missing little boy. Danny Turner, have you ever heard the name before?" I asked, getting straight to the point.

Singleton looked at me and pursed his lips as though deeply pondering the name, "No, no, the name doesn't ring a bell. Why...should it? What would I know about a missing little boy by that name?" he asked confidently with a frown.

"That's what I'm trying to find out. Let me try another name on you; Ruben LaPorte. Does that name ring a bell?"

The name of LaPorte certainly got his attention, "Ruben, yes I know Ruben LaPorte. We're acquainted anyway."

"You mean you were acquainted, don't you?" I said watching his reaction closely.

"What do you mean, 'were acquainted?' Has something happened to Ruben?" Singleton asked, much more curious now.

"Yeah, something happened to him all right. He went swimming in a place that didn't have a lifeguard on duty...his bathtub," I said firmly.

"You mean he slipped in his tub...is he...dead?"

"He's dead all right, but he didn't slip. He was held under the water."

Singleton's eyes widened noticeably. He moved over to a chair and sat down. I could see he was obviously shaken. So much for casual acquaintances, I thought to myself.

"How close were you and Ruben LaPorte, Mr. Singleton?" I asked.

"Actually we were much closer than casual acquaintances, Mr. Castle, but then I guess you already knew that, didn't you?"

"I had an idea, seeing as how you worked at the same medical clinic in the LA area. Who would want to see him dead? Do you have any idea?"

Singleton exhaled loudly as he looked towards the floor and shook his head slowly, "No, not off hand. Well, Ruben could be quite combative at times, so I guess someone he had a run-in with might like to see harm come to him," he said and then looked up at me quickly. "You're not suggesting that I had something to do with it, are you?" he asked.

"I'm not suggesting anything; I'm just asking questions. Questions, I'd say, that the cops are going to be asking as well. They may even want to know what you know about Norma Turner and her son, Danny," I pressed.

"Norma Turner...Norma Turner? Now that you mention it, Mr. Castle I do remember Ruben talking about a Norma Turner. I believe she was a patient at the institution where he works, uh, worked. Yes, yes, that's it. She was a patient there. He talked about her because she had a baby while she was there," he offered.

Now it was my turn to look shocked. If he was telling the truth I was just handed the football on the goal line and could carry it over for a touchdown. All I had to do now was not fumble it.

"That's what he told you, huh? That she had a baby while she was a patient there? You don't recall when he told you that do you?"

"Let's see, yes, I do as a matter of fact. It was the night of my birthday party and one of the guests asked him what he was doing now and he made the statement that he'd just helped deliver a baby. That was how the whole conversation came about and the reason I still remember it. He was quite excited about it seeing as how it was his first time at seeing a delivery as well as actually helping with it."

"So how long ago was it?" I asked since he had not given me a date or time line.

"That was the year I moved into this house. Just about five years ago now," he paused. "Rueben's dead; it's hard to imagine."

Just then Singleton's butler opened the library door and looked in. Singleton and I both looked in the butler's direction.

"Excuse me, Sir, but your guests said they were going to go upstairs and change into their swimsuits and take a dip in the pool. They asked me to inform you," the butler said properly.

"Okay, Charles, I'll be joining them shortly. As soon as I'm finished with Mr. Castle," Singleton said looking hopefully at me.

"I'm just about through with my questions, Mr. Singleton. If I were you, though, I'd be prepared to answer them again as soon as the police get around to you," I replied.

"Yes, I suppose they will. Do you have anymore questions for me?" he asked.

"No...not right now I don't. If I should have other questions is there a number I can call you at to save me a trip back out here. It's a little less intrusive over the phone," I asked.

"Yes, here's my card. You can call me at either of the numbers on it. I should be at one or the other."

"Thank you for your time, Mr. Singleton. I'm sorry to have been the bearer of bad news, but you would have heard sooner or later," I said apologetically.

Just then the phone rang and Singleton moved to the large desk and picked up the receiver.

"Hello, this Theo," he said easily.

He paused for a few seconds, "Yes, I know, I was just informed," he said and looked at me.

"No, not the police, a private investigator," he said with a smile that told me the caller was informing him of LaPorte's murder.

"How did you find out about it so soon, Cory?" he asked, which was what I was wondering myself.

"Oh, you stopped by to pick him up to go golfing, huh?" Theodore stated for my benefit.

I nodded in recognition and then motioned towards the door, indicating that I'd see myself out, which got an agreeable nod from him.

I walked to the door and opened it pausing just long enough to look back. Singleton turned to face the door as I exited. I walked out and closed the door behind me. Waiting just long enough to let Singleton think I'd gone, I reopened the door a crack, just enough to be able to hear what he was saying to whomever it was that had called. Obviously Singleton had not noticed the door was ajar.

"He knew about LaPorte and me working together. But what is more disturbing than that is what he was asking about the Turner woman. I told you that this was going to get out of hand. I want out of this and I mean...wait just a minute," Singleton said.

I knew it was time for me to make a hasty retreat and didn't waste anytime moving speedily on tiptoes away from the door. By the time Singleton had opened the door to check on my whereabouts I was just opening the front door where I stopped and looked back as if to say, 'Was there something else?' He smiled and nodded another goodbye and then closed the door, unaware that I'd overheard his end of the conversation.

It would be obvious to even the most novice investigator that Singleton was involved in this case up to his evenly plucked eyebrows. I was reasonably sure that he hadn't heard of LaPorte's murder until he heard it from me. As far as the phone call from the man he called Cory, I doubted very seriously that the man had stopped by LaPorte's to take him golfing. I had to think the reason he stopped was more sinister than stomping around a golf course somewhere.

There's no explaining why I hadn't driven away from Singleton's home as soon as I reached my car, but I didn't. I had sat there deep in thought for several minutes before starting the engine. When I did, I casually looked up at one of the upstairs windows.

A woman was standing at the window and looking out over the immaculately manicured landscape. She was beautiful as the sun reflected off the window glass and formed a sort of halo around her dark hair. I noticed a sort of lonely look on the woman's face; a face that was very familiar to me; a face, I might add that I had tenderly held in my hands as I kissed the sweet, pliant lips of the woman to whom the face belonged. The face at that time belonged to one Miss Karen Ferris; but more recently had been changed to Karen Ciccarelli.

CHAPTER

8

S TUNNED BY THE SUDDEN realization that the woman in the window was none other than the woman I'd been in love with a few years earlier is an understatement. I literally rubbed my eyes to make sure I was seeing clearly. Looking again, however, only made me more certain that it was indeed Karen. Then the questions, who, what, when, where, and why?

Why was she here at Theodore Singleton's home? What was she doing here? When had she met Singleton? Where had she come from and with who, or is it whom? My mind raced as I continued to stare up at the window. Karen never looked my way; she seemed to be a million miles away.

I wanted to call to her, or go back inside and see her, or honk the horn, but did none of those things. Instead I just sat there and stared. After maybe thirty seconds Karen turned and moved away from the window, leaving me with a sick feeling in the pit of my stomach.

There're some things a person just seems to know without any evidence whatsoever. It's just something that seems to be revealed to you. That was my feeling towards Theodore

Singleton. This man was dirty from the top of his carefully styled hair to the soles of his size seven to seven and a half size feet. It made me sick to think that Karen may be involved in something, make that anything, this guy was involved in.

The name Ciccarelli popped into my head like a flashing neon light. That was the name that I'd been told was now Karen's married name. What had Carl said about the man Karen had married; something about being rich? Maybe I'd better check out his name and see what I could find out. Then I asked myself another question; did I want to know the answers because of the Turner case, or for my own information? I honestly couldn't say.

As I headed back towards the city and Norma Turner's house, I had several questions that I wanted to put directly to her. She was holding something back from me and I knew she'd held it back from the police as well. There were just too many blank spots in what she'd told me and what I was learning through my investigation. I could certainly see why the police had more or less dropped her case.

I dialed Norma's number and was relieved when she answered the phone. I told her I was on my way over to see her and was told that she'd be expecting me. When I arrived I saw Earl Cromwell's car parked in the driveway so I pulled up to the curb.

Norma opened the door before I ever reached it. She had a much more worried look on her face now than she had before, as she held the door open for me to enter. I gave her a stern look as I passed her and moved into the living room. Earl was sitting in an easy chair, but stood up when I entered the room, a deeper look of worry on his face than he'd worn before. Something was up, but I was not expecting what I was about to hear.

"Mr. Castle, Danny is missing," Norma said nearly in tears.

Was she having another breakdown? Why was she restating the obvious?

"Yes, I know he's missing. That's why you hired me, remember?" I said easily, my irate-ness subsiding drastically.

"No, I mean, yes...oh, I mean he's really missing this time," Norma said as tears began to stream down her face.

I looked at Earl and the look on his face told me that something was definitely amiss here. Quickly I looked back at Norma Turner and felt my anger rising slightly as I began to feel I'd been left in the dark about a number of things.

"All right, what's going on here," I snapped. "I need some answers, Mrs. Turner, and I need them now. If you want me to continue on with this case you're going to have to do some explaining. Now what's going on?" I said coming straight to the point.

After a quick look in Earl's direction which drew a nod of his head as he said quietly, "You'd better tell him everything, honey."

Norma took a deep breath and sighed resignedly as she answered, "My son has really been kidnapped this time."

"This time...what do you mean this time? Are you telling me he wasn't kidnapped before?" I said trying not to show how stunned I was at the statement.

"Yes, that's what I'm saying," Norma said ashamedly.

"So he wasn't really kidnapped when you went to the police the first time?"

"No, that was all a plan to make certain people think he had been kidnapped," Norma stated which drew another admission from Earl.

"That was my idea, Mr. Castle," he said.

"Okay, hold it. Let's go back to the beginning and start from there because I'm about one wrong word from walking away from here...no, let me rephrase that; from 'running' away from here as fast as I can."

"Okay, Mr. Castle, I'll tell you everything, but please don't leave the case, I beg you," Norma pleaded.

"That all depends on what you tell me right now. Let's start with the question I was going to ask you as soon as I got here, and then you take it from there, okay?" I snapped.

"Okay, I'll tell you everything," Norma said and sat down on the sofa.

"Where was your son, your second son, Danny; where was he born; in which hospital?"

Norma looked down and then raised her eyes to meet mine, "I don't know."

"You don't know? You mean you don't know where your own son was born? I'd think that a mother would know those things. You were present, were you not," I said facetiously?

She looked hurt, scared, and confused all at the same time, which caused me to wish I hadn't been so stern with her, "I was totally out of it when Danny was born."

Norma took a deep breath and then went on, "Mr. Castle, I kidnapped Danny from the people that stole him from me. And then I faked his kidnapping, and now he's missing and I think the ones that took him when he was a baby have him again."

Now it was my turn to look confused, "What? I think you'd better explain this whole thing to me...and in great detail."

Norma straightened herself as if someone preparing to make a long speech and sorting out their notes for easy reference. In her case, however, she was sorting things out in her mind, and I hoped it was a sound mind.

"Mr. Castle, as you know, I was institutionalized for sometime after I lost my first little boy, who was also named Danny. My loss, my guilt, and my shame were simply too much for me to handle and I snapped. When I went to the hospital I was, to put it mildly, a basket case. The hospital staff had me on suicide watch for the first couple of months I was there.

"After I had been there for several months, they began to increase the medications they had me on until I couldn't remember anything at all about those days. I walked around as though in a dream or trance like state. Nothing made any sense to me, because in my mind I couldn't tell what was actually happening from what I might be dreaming; it was all so surreal.

"I was allowed no visitors during that time, something I learned after being discharged from there. But I knew that something had happened that was not merely a dream. Something's are just too real to hide with drugs. I knew I had had a baby while in there.

"The hospital denied it, naturally, but I knew that I had had a baby. I began to have flashbacks that helped convince me, but the doctor attending me said it was just illusions due to the fact that I had lost my own little boy, coupled with the medication they had me on. As they cut my medications, though, I knew better.

"When I got out of the hospital I contacted my sister, Kirsten Johns, and she came to stay with me for a few weeks. I told her of my feelings and she began to ask questions at the hospital where I'd been. The doctor that had attended me after Dr. Berg left, tried to convince her that it was just the effects of the drugs they had me on, but she didn't go along with it and hired a private investigator; a man by the name of Steven Wilcox.

"He began to investigate, but suddenly quit, saying there was nothing to report. We read a short time later that he was killed when he drove his car over a cliff along Highway 1 near Devil's Slide."

I remembered the case very well. The police suspected foul play, but were unable to come up with anything.

Norma continued, "I began to have dreams that were much like the dreams I had had when institutionalized only now it was more like true flashbacks to something that had actually happened. I kept seeing the face of a man as he inserted an instrument," she paused and looked quickly at Earl, "up...inside me; if you know what I mean. The man's face began to grow more defined as the dreams became clearer, until I realized he was a doctor there in the hospital."

I took a chance and cut in on her, "Rueben LaPorte?" I asked.

Norma looked surprised when I mentioned his name, "No, not him, but he was present. But, how did you know about LaPorte?"

"Let's just say it goes along with some of the things he was involved in earlier in his checkered past. Go ahead with your story."

I didn't tell her right away that LaPorte had been murdered, not wanting to interfere with the emotional soul cleansing she was going through. I'd tell her after she had related everything she could about her recollections of the past.

"Anyway, Kirsten had to go home and Earl took over looking into things that had happened during my stay in the hospital. He hired a man that he knows that is a..." she paused as she looked in Earl's direction.

"It's okay, honey, go ahead and tell him," Earl said, giving his okay to what Norma was about to say."

"The man is a burglar for hire. He will break into places and gather whatever the person that hires him wants and probably helps himself to whatever he wants, as well. Anyway, he found a file folder that contained everything about me...and the little boy I gave birth to while in the hospital."

The look on my face must have gone from being very attentive to one of total shock. I had been right about her possibly having had a baby while institutionalized, but hearing the actual words coming from the woman involved still came as somewhat of a surprise.

She went on, "The man that Earl hired also found a file on my new little Danny. The people involved had sold him to a couple that lives in Hillsborough; obviously they have money. We now had the name and address of the people that had bought my baby and I knew if I could only see him, I'd know in my heart if he belonged to me or not. The moment I saw him, Mr. Castle, something told me that he was my little boy.

"A birth certificate in my son's file bore the names of the couple in Hillsborough as being the natural parents and it also bore the name Danny as the name of the baby. Earl said that was so the police would think I was still having emotional problems if I ever went to them talking about having a little boy named Danny. They would just think it was a mad woman talking about the little boy she'd lost. I guess Earl was right."

I digested everything that she was telling me and for the first time this case began to make some real sense. The fact that she hadn't been up front with the police even made a little sense now, as well. If she told them this story; in her mind, anyway, she was afraid she might be in trouble for kidnapping her own son and she didn't want to take that kind of chance. She may have also feared the ones involved in the baby selling organization might do her, or her baby, physical harm.

Norma went on to explain why she'd enrolled Danny into elementary school and Sunday school and then didn't let him attend. She said she knew that if the ones involved in the baby selling ring figured she had taken the boy, they would be watching her house and would probably even have the school staked out. Little Danny was actually living at Earl Cromwell's house and Norma had moved enough of her things in there that she could spend time between the two places.

She said that Earl and she had worked out a good scheme for losing anyone that might be tailing her, so she was sure no one had followed her to Earl's. It sounded plausible to Norma and Earl, but I knew that it would just be a matter of time until professionals would figure everything out and grab the boy. It looked like that time had come.

"But now they've taken Danny. I guess they must have followed me without my knowing it and learned that he was with Earl. Earl called just after you did today and told me that Danny was gone. He'd been playing in the back yard and when Earl looked out after a few minutes, the back gate was standing wide open and Danny was gone," Norma said and began to cry again.

I thought for a second before trying to calm her down, "Danny may not have been grabbed by them, then. He may have wandered out the back gate and be somewhere in the neighborhood. Did you check that possibility out, Earl?"

"Yes, but I know someone took him, Mr. Castle. I had been in the back yard with him and went inside for just a minute and when I came back he was gone. That old gate is heavy and you have to lift it up off the post it rests on, because one of the hinges is broken. Danny couldn't have lifted it up; that would take someone bigger and stronger," Earl explained.

"I see. Well, we'll find him; I'm sure of that. Let me get something cleared up here. Was Danny with you the day you reported him missing at the shopping center?" I asked, somewhat sure of what the answer would be.

"No, in fact, he was with Earl. There was no kidnapping. I was afraid that the people that had sold him would come looking for him if they suspected that I might be the one that had taken him, so I made up the kidnapping story so they would think someone else had taken him. There would be no sense in following me around if they believed someone had kidnapped him from me," she explained.

I thought for a few seconds, "Where's the files that the man lifted from the hospital?"

"My sister Kirsten that lives in Washington is sending them by registered mail. We felt that if she kept them no one would be able to get their hands on them. Did we do the right thing?" Norma asked.

"No, you didn't. You should have gone to the police with the files and the entire story and exposed this bunch of thieves to them. By not telling the police the whole story, they were left to think exactly what they did; especially when they found out that you'd lost your first little boy named Danny. Naturally they figured that you were still suffering from mental problems," I paused. "Is that why you told me you would have proof there was a second boy named Danny, because your sister had to mail the files down here to you?"

"Yes, they should be here today sometime. What will you do with the files, Mr. Castle?" Norma asked haltingly.

"Two things; first I'm going to go to the address in Hillsborough and see if your son has been taken back there. The second thing I'm going to do is talk to a friend of mine with the police.

"To be honest, Mrs. Turner, I doubt that your son is in the house at Hillsborough. If they somehow learned of Danny's whereabouts and snatched him from you, I would imagine that they're keeping him in another location. What I want to do before alerting the police is see if I can locate him and get him back to you before the police move in. Don't worry though, we'll get him back."

I could see the tension and worry drain slightly from Norma's face. The worry lines relaxed and a sincere, unforced smile came to her face for the first time since I'd met her.

"What are the names of the people that had Danny living with them?" I asked.

"Wingate; Mr. and Mrs. Lloyd Wingate; her first name is Camille."

Earl interjected at that time, "I had him checked out and found that he's an attorney in San Francisco. From what I was able to find out, Mrs. Wingate had to have a hysterectomy years ago and therefore is unable to bear children. They wouldn't be able to adopt legally because of something that happened when Mr. Wingate was twenty one and was caught sexually molesting a fifteen year old girl. With that on his record he would never be approved for legal adoption. I guess that's how they wound up involved with this baby selling ring."

"Well, I can tell you this, Earl; he's going to have another black mark on his record when this story breaks. More than likely he'll be disbarred and go to prison, which he obviously deserves."

"What about Mrs. Wingate," Norma asked in a concerned voice, "You don't think she'll be in any trouble do you?"

I could see the worry in her eyes for the wellbeing of the woman that had stolen her baby from her. I guess it was something only a mother could understand.

"It all depends, Mrs. Turner. If she knowingly participated in the transaction, she probably will be charged with being a willing accomplice in the crime. I don't really see how she could not have known about it; unless, her husband did all the dealings without her knowledge, then she would not be held responsible, I guess."

"I hope she didn't know. I can just imagine how much she wanted to have a baby," she paused, "And Danny was well taken care of; I'm sure she loved him a lot."

"Well, that's a matter for the courts to work out. Our main objective now is to locate him and get him back to you."

Before I left Norma's UPS dropped off the files that Kirsten had sent down from her home in Washington. I told Norma that it would be best if I kept the files with me. She agreed and I prepared to leave and take the files to my office where I'd make sure they were safely filed away.

When I got to the door I had another thought about something I wanted to get cleared up.

"What about the two men that were parked next to me the other day when you drove up outside here? I take it you'd seen them before, am I right?" I asked.

"Yes, they have followed us a number of times. They went around to our neighbors asking them if they'd ever seen a little boy here at my house, and since the neighbors hadn't they told them so. I thought they might stop hanging around, but they didn't. The neighbors haven't seen little Danny because we took him straight to Earl's the day we grabbed him," Norma explained.

For a couple of rank amateurs Norma and Earl hadn't done too badly, but considering the fact that someone had grabbed the boy was proof they'd obviously miscalculated. I wanted to get back to the office and run some checks on the Wingate family. The name actually rang a bell with me, but I couldn't remember for what. I knew it would come to me before long, though; it usually did.

I drove straight to the office, but checked my rearview mirror constantly. I certainly didn't want someone following me and getting the files I had back. These files meant arrest warrants for the individuals involved and I figured there was nothing they wouldn't do to get them. I didn't know how right I was until I noticed the black sedan pull out from behind a rental truck some six cars behind me and start speeding up alongside my car.

CHAPTER

9

THE SEDAN SPED UP alongside mine and I noticed the window on the passenger's side start rolling down. I saw the muzzle of what appeared to be a shotgun emerge through the window and knew that these were not hunter's going out to shoot game birds.

I hit the accelerator and sped up behind the car ahead of me as though I was going to run right over it. Just before our bumpers collided, however, I swerved into the right lane, cutting off a tractor and trailer. I heard the truck lockup its breaks and I tromped on the gas pedal as if trying to shove my foot through the floor board.

When I came to the next exit I took it and made a sharp left at the bottom of the ramp. I didn't wait for the light to change, but I could see far enough to know there wasn't a car anywhere near the intersection.

As soon as I passed under the freeway I took a hard left onto the on ramp of the freeway I had just exited, but going in the opposite direction. I didn't spare the horses as I raced up the on ramp into much lighter traffic. It was only then that I ventured a glance in the mirror to see if my pursuers were still on my tail. They weren't, so I slowed considerably. I exited the freeway at the third exit I came to, keeping a watchful eye on my rear view mirror the entire time. I stuck to side streets as I headed in the direction of my office. It took me a lot longer this way, but it made it easier to make sure I didn't pick up the tail again.

It was a little after three o'clock in the afternoon by the time I pulled into the parking lot across the street from my office. As I locked my car and started across the lot I noticed the same dark colored sedan parked in an alleyway just up the street. The car was sitting in such a way that the occupants would be able to see the front of the building as well as anyone coming or going from the parking lot.

I put my hand inside my coat and merely touched the grip of my .38 snub nosed revolver that was in the shoulder holster. Just knowing the hardware was there gave me a sense of security.

Keeping a sharp eye on the dark sedan I darted between cars on the somewhat busy street without any trouble. No one emerged from the sedan and due to the tinted windows I could not tell if there was anyone sitting in it. The thought crossed my mind that one of the men might be inside the office building, while the other waited in the car.

Before entering the building I checked the lobby area for any suspicious looking characters that might be hanging around there. I didn't see anyone that looked like they might want to use me for target practice, so I went inside.

With my eyes scanning the lobby area I hurried to the elevators and turned so my back was against the wall. Nothing seemed amiss so I punched the up button and waited for one of the three cars to arrive. I was relieved when the middle elevator door opened and its occupants exited. I stepped inside and pushed the button for my floor.

Just as the elevator's doors were closing I saw two men enter the building. Although I wasn't one hundred percent sure, I thought it might be the two behemoths that had roughed me up in the garage at my condominium and that I'd roughed up outside Norma Turner's place.

When I reached my floor I hurried down the hall to my office door and stepped inside, but didn't close the door all the way. I stood holding the door open just a crack so I could watch the elevator doors. Myrna was busy typing a letter to a prospective client, but when she saw me, she stopped.

"What is it, Nick; you look like someone's after you?" she asked.

"I think someone is after me, Myrna. In fact I'm expecting them to show up any time now. You might want to slip out of here, Honey. Use the stairs and be quick about it; there could be some gunplay," I said seriously.

Myrna didn't waste any time at all in grabbing her purse and coat and making a hasty exit from the office. But not before she got off one of her patented remarks.

"I'll see you tomorrow, Nick; one way or the other," she said, but then added quickly, "Do you want me to call someone...like the police?"

"No, I'll handle these two boys myself," I reassured her.

Myrna hurried down the hallway towards the stairs. I waited until she'd disappeared through the doorway before setting up my little surprise for Twiddle Dee and Twiddle Dumb.

I looked around the room for something that could be used to my advantage. The first thing I noticed was Myrna's large knitting basket sitting by her desk. She liked to knit when there was some slack time and left her knitting basket here during the week, only taking it home with her on weekends.

The second thing I noticed was the table mounted vise in one corner of the room. Michael had mounted the vise on the table when he worked on his pistol, or little projects he brought with him from home; these being household gadgets of one kind or another.

I hurriedly pulled my .38 from my shoulder holster and mounted it in the vice with the barrel aimed in the direction of the door. Rushing to Myrna's knitting bag I grabbed a skein of yarn and quickly unrolled enough to reach from the door knob to the gun mounted in the vise. Quickly I wrapped the yarn around the handle of the door and ran it across the room to the gun. I tied the string around the trigger and then cocked the hammer back on the .38

I checked the mirror I had installed above the office door so I can see who comes out of the elevators and just as I did the doors opened and the two escapees from the WWF (World Wrestling Federation) stepped out. One of the men was carrying something wrapped in newspaper and holding it under one arm. I figured it to be the shotgun or rifle he'd aimed at me from the car window earlier.

The two men checked the room numbers that were either stenciled directly on the door windows or tacked above the doors on the frame. They started down the hallway the wrong way, but quickly changed direction. They were looking for my office all right, but I would be ready for them.

By this time the two men were nearing my office door. I'd have to work fast. I ran to my office and grabbed my .357 Magnum out of my desk drawer, just as I got back to the door that led to the outer office the .38 discharged. I heard a scream of pain and looked through the open door just in time to see the man with the newspaper wrapped shotgun doubled over. The other man opened fire in the direction of the pistol mounted on the table.

I fired three shots in rapid succession through the door and heard a loud yell, a dead sounding thud, and then total silence. Cautiously I moved across the room to where the first man was lying on the floor. He wasn't dead, but close to it.

After kicking the gun out of his reach I checked on the second shooter.

The second man had been hit by two of the three slugs that had blown holes in my office door. He was dead; his eyes wide open in a stunned stare. I recognized the two of them by their size, first off, and secondly by their faces. It was Big Foot and his brother Goliath; the two goons I'd had run-ins with before; there was no doubt about it.

By this time people from the adjoining business offices were looking out their office doors, albeit cautiously. The CPA just down the hall from our office was the first to call out.

"Say Nick, are you all right?" he asked as he stuck half his face around the door frame.

"Yeah, I'm okay Donald," I replied. "I'll call the police and get this mess cleaned up."

Now people were coming out of the offices in droves. Some merely peeked at the bodies and quickly turned away, while the more curious looked at them from all sides. I had to warn them not to touch anything until the police got here and did their work. I went back inside my office and untied the string from the door handle and took the .38 out of the vise. As far as the police were concerned I'd been firing with a gun in each hand. It wasn't long before the place was swarming with cops.

I went through the usual question and answer routine, explaining how these two guys had roughed me up once and tried to gun me on the freeway earlier. I got the obligatory lecture about calling the police when in danger, which I countered with the question, "And you truly believe these two would have waited until you got here to start firing at me?"

After making a statement and being told not to leave town, I was aloud to leave so the cleanup boys could do their job. When I cleared the building I gave John Hernandez a call and told him what had happened. He said he knew there had been a shooting in my office building, and pretty much figured I had to be involved somehow.

"You might want to see if you can tie these two goons to the Ruben LaPorte murder, John. I think they're involved in something that LaPorte was a major player in," I said, intentionally holding back what I now knew for certain about the baby selling racket.

"Would you care to reveal your source of information on this, Nick?" John asked.

"I will, but not right now. I can tell you this, though, John. Mrs. Turner isn't off her nut; not anymore. There really is a little boy named Danny. I've seen his birth certificate; at least one with his name on it," I offered.

"You're on to something, aren't you, Nick? Be careful my friend. You don't want to start withholding information from us," John said, issuing a friendly warning.

"Hey, you guys had this thing on a back burner in the back room of a backwoods cabin, so don't act like this was an ongoing investigation, John. You told me yourself that you didn't actually think there was a little boy, remember," I replied harshly.

"Yeah, yeah, but if there's new evidence we can move that case from the back burner of the backwoods cabin back yonder in the backwoods where...ah, wherever you said we had the case," John groused.

I laughed and then made my old friend feel better as I tossed him a bone, "John, I'll keep you abreast of any thing new as they turn up. Right now there're just a lot of educated guesses, but they're beginning to come together making a nice, neat little picture. If something solid turns up you'll be the first to know," I said reassuringly.

"You'll keep me *abreast* of things? I love it when you talk sexy to me, Nick. Okay, Pahdna, I'll take your word for it. But be careful, would you? I don't want to be attending your funeral. It looks to me like these guy's play rough and play for keeps."

"You're right there. Take it easy, Johnny."

"You too, Nicky," John said and hung up.

CHAPTER

10

MYRNA LOOKED AT THE DOOR to the office and shook her head, "How many times do I have to tell you to use the door handle, Nick. Don't just walk up and try to push the door open without turning the little knob down here," she said jokingly with wide eyes. "Boy, Nick, you meant business, didn't you."

"I didn't have a chance to do anything else, Myrna. It was either them or me. I'm just glad it was them," I replied, and then added. "Oh, by the way, I borrowed some of your yarn and believe me; I will never say another word about you knitting here in the office."

"How much did you use?" Myrna asked with a slight frown.

"I didn't use that much, Myrna. Just enough to reach from the door to the vise that Michael mounted on the table over there. The vise I gave him such a hard time about, remember?"

"What were you doing with my yarn and his vise when two guys are about to cancel your life's ticket?" Myrna asked, but quickly added, "On second thought, I don't even want to know."

"I've already called maintenance and they will have a guy up here sometime this morning to put a new door on. If I'm not here make sure they spell Michael's name right. I don't want a mess like we had when he came onboard as a partner. Remember?" I asked with a smile

"Don't I? Let's see, first they put Micah Bishop; then it was Micah Bushop; and finally, Michele Bishop. They finally got it right on the fourth try. Yeah, I remember," Myrna laughed.

"I'll be going out to see Mrs. Turner in case the police call. If they do, give them my cell phone number. I should be back this afternoon sometime. Oh, and if Michael calls with any news find out the phone number where he can be reached. I doubt that his cell phone will do any good down there."

"Okay, Nick. Have a good day. Oh, and while I'm thinking of it, which skein did you take the yarn from?"

I looked at her with a puzzled look on my face, "The white one, why?"

"Just wanted you to remember when you pick another one up for me," she said matter-of-factly. I frowned, but it turned into a grin as I walked out the door and headed for the elevator.

I had a couple of more questions I wanted to talk to Norma Turner about. I'd called her from my home and set a time for our meeting. Before I was to meet her, however, I wanted to talk to an old friend of mine. If anyone could tell me about a baby selling racket going on in town, he would be the man. He had his nose in everything.

I called Larry Worthington's home number, but didn't get an answer so I figured I'd try some of his old haunts. It been sometime since I'd actually seen Larry, but I'd talked to him on the phone a number of times over the past six months.

My first stop was Vinny Damon's Billiards Parlor. Vinny was an ex-pool hustler that had opened his own place when a couple of sore losers broke his thumbs and fingers after he'd taken them for a bundle. Now he let the other guys do the playing and he just watched.

Vinny was sitting behind the counter reading a racing form when I entered his place of business. Looking over the top of the form his eyes crinkled from the smile that came to his face. Vinny and I went back to my days on the force. I'd saved him from a mugging by three guys after he'd had a successful night of 9 ball shooting. He'd never forgotten and always seemed happy to see me.

"Hey, Vinny; how's tricks?" I said as we shook hands.

"Same old rabbit out of the hat trick; you can't beat that one," Vinny said, giving his standard reply to that particular question.

"You haven't seen Larry Worthington around lately have you?" I asked as I turned and scoured the four billiards and six pool tables, only three of which had anyone playing on them.

"Yeah, he's right over there," Vinny said as he pointed at a pool table that had two men playing at it. "He was there, anyway," Vinny continued when he saw that Larry was no longer there.

"Maybe he went to the john, I'll wait a minute," I said and turned back towards Vinny. "Give me a cup of coffee while I'm waiting, Vinny," I said and tossed a dollar on the counter.

"On the house, Nick," Vinny replied and poured me a cup of black coffee into a thick tan coffee mug.

'Thanks, Vinny. So, are you still single or did you tie the knot since I saw you last?"

"Still foot loose and fancy free. No, marriage and I don't get along, Nick...mainly because my wives and I didn't get along."

Raymond D. Mason

"You just haven't found your right mate yet, Vinny. Miss Right is out there, just keep looking," I said as I took a sip of the strong hot coffee.

"That's the problem, Nick. I've been finding Miss Wrong all these years. I should have figured that out," Vinny joked.

Just then he looked past me in the direction of the restrooms.

"There's Larry, now. I guess he was in the washroom," Vinny stated.

Looking in Larry's direction I noticed that he'd lost a couple of pounds since the last time I'd seen him. He looked trim and was well dressed. I took my coffee and moved away from the counter towards Larry. When he recognized me he stopped dead in his tracks.

"Nick...I hear you escaped a close call yesterday?" Larry stated.

"How'd you find that out so fast?" I asked truly surprised at how fast news traveled, especially news of this nature.

"Say, I knew about it with an hour after it happened. Any idea who it was that tried to gun you?"

"I was hoping you might be able to shed some light on that, Larry?" I replied.

Larry blew his cheeks out as he took in a lung full of air and then held it in his mouth as he slowly exhaled; something he did when he was thinking. I figured he was either trying to come up with the names of people that might be involved, or, he was trying to decide if he should tell me what he knew about the attempt on my life. All I could do was wait and see what his decision would be.

Finally he made up his mind, "The word on the street is that you've taken up the Turner woman's case, is that right?" he asked.

"Yeah, Norma Turner, the one that lost the little boy," I replied easily.

Larry scratched his head, "Have you heard of a man by the name of Julian Rossi?"

"Rossi, no, the name doesn't ring a bell, Larry? Who is he?"

"Julian Rossi is a man you don't want to mess with, my friend. Julian, or Julie, as some of his more intimate friends call him, is an 'Out of Towner' that has his fingers in so many shady dealings in the city that he should be an 'In Towner.' His biggest and most shady business right now, is the baby market. The word has it that he's unhappy with your nosing around on this Turner case."

"Where's this guy live, Larry; or does it matter?"

"It matters, believe me. He lives in Washington, D. C. where he runs a stable of call girls that visit our illustrious political leaders on a regular basis. Rossi has so much dirt on these elected bozos that they can't scratch without his permission. If he wants a bill passed, it gets passed...and with flying colors, I might add."

"So how does this tie him in with the baby selling racket?" I asked.

"This man is diversified. He's got his tentacles into more businesses than an ocean full of octopuses. The word is that Norma Turner was one of those that 'got away' if you get my drift."

"Come on, Larry, you're not trying to tell me that this bunch gets women pregnant while they're in a hospital somewhere and then sell the baby, are you," I said unbelievingly.

"That's right; artificial insemination. From what I hear Rossi's kid sister received Norma Turner's baby."

My heart skipped a beat when I heard this. I threw a name at Larry in hopes he'd heard it. "His sister's name wouldn't be Camille, would it, Larry?"

Now it was Larry's turn to look surprised. He grinned, "Yeah, Camille Wingate. Her husband's name is...," Larry replied.

I cut him off before he could say Mr. Wingate's first name, "Lloyd."

"You've got it Dick Tracy. Camille can't have children because of a botched abortion when she was younger, but Lloyd can, and from what I heard, did have one; it was his sperm they used to impregnate Norma Turner," Larry paused. Nick...keep your back covered because Julian Rossi is bad medicine. He carries a lot of weight, or muscle, or whatever you want to call it."

"I owe you, Larry. Here's a twenty and you have a steak dinner coming," I said as I fished out a twenty dollar bill and handed it to him.

"You don't have to do this, Nick, but thanks," Larry said as he took the money and quickly shoved it into his pants pocket.

"Later, pardner," I said and walked out.

This case was turning into a can of worms, but those are the kind of cases I love. The roots of evil go deep; all the way to hell and where there's dirt, all kinds of evil grows there. As is usually the case, where there's evil, there's money involved somewhere. You can't deny the truth in the Scripture, "The love of money is the root of all evil."

The sons of Satan that deal in filthy businesses all do it for one reason; the money, and nothing is too low for them. Murder, robbery, illicit sex, the selling of illegal drugs that destroys not only the addict, but entire families as well, are all spawned by the love of money. It sounded to me like Julian Rossi was one of those sons of whom Satan must be very proud.

I'd never heard Julian Rossi's name before, but I was sure that my good friend John Hernandez had. Maybe a call on

John could get me a little more lowdown on this Rossi creep. I called John on my cell phone and invited him to lunch.

Lt. Hernandez had already gotten a table and was waiting for me when I arrived at Luigi's Italian Restaurant. I made my way through the throng of lunchtime diners that always crowded into the small restaurant during the week. The tables all had red and white checkered table cloths and a wine bottle with a candle in it sitting in the middle of it which added to the Old World décor.

"What kept you, Nick? I'm starving...you are buying right?" John asked with a grin.

"Hey, with what I'm about to lay on you, you should be buying," I replied with my own grin.

"What's new on the Turner case?"

"A lot, John; first I have to ask you a question. What do you know about a guy by the name of Julian Rossi; he's from the D. C. area from what I hear?" I questioned.

John frowned, "What does he have to do with the Turner case?"

"Have you heard of him?"

"Yeah, I've heard of him. Look in the dictionary under 'sleaze ball' and you'll find his picture. Does he have something to do with the Turner woman?"

"Not with her, with the hospital she was in. In fact, his baby sister's husband is probably the father of Norma Turner's baby," I said and waited for John's reaction.

"Give me the whole story, Nick," John said seriously.

"Hang onto your hat, because this is a little confusing," I said, preparing John for the story I was about to share with him.

I related most of what Norma Turner had told me about little Danny's birth, kidnapping by her and Earl, faking the kidnapping, and now the real kidnapping that had taken place. When I finished John sat there with his mouth slightly agape and a dumbfounded look on his face. He shut his eyes and slowly shook his head.

"I should have taken up taxidermy like my dad told me too. This is bizarre to say the least, Nick. Let me get this straight. First Norma Turner goes to the hospital with a nervous breakdown; they impregnate her; she has the baby; they sell the baby to the father and his wife; the baby is stolen by Mrs. Turner when she learns the truth, then she fakes a kidnapping to throw them off her tracks, and now the little guy is really kidnapped again? Do I have it right?"

"That's it, Johnny; that's it in a nutshell."

"Why don't you stick to divorce cases, Nick? Your cases are always so...complicated."

"Hey, you guys started this one, remember. I just picked it up when you stopped looking for the little tyke. We now know that Norma Turner is not a fruitcake and with what she can tell us, this bunch of black market baby dealers are headed up the river. I say let the dragnet begin."

"We want to make sure we get the ringleaders though, Nick. We don't want to move too fast and drive the brains and big money boys underground. Rossi may not be the brains behind the business, or even part of the business. It could be that his sister is the only reason he's involved," John said thoughtfully.

"If he's the one that sent the two goons after me, though, he's got more at stake than just trying to get little Danny back for his sister. No, I figure he's got to be a major player in this thing. Of course, I may be wrong," I argued.

Just then the waitress came and took our order. We'd already been there fifteen minutes, but you expected a long wait for everything when you ate at Luigi's. The food made the wait well worthwhile. We continued to discuss the case over lunch and when we'd finished took our conversation outside to John's car that was parallel parked at the curb just down from the restaurant.

"Where do you think the boy might be, Nick?" John asked.

"I don't know, John. I don't think he's at the Wingate's, though. They wouldn't be foolish enough to take him back there. I don't think. They've got to figure that's the first place that Norma Turner would send the police. I really don't know where they might have taken the boy." I paused as I thought of something, "But, I'll check the Wingate's out and let you know what I find out."

"Okay, but you didn't tell me what you were going to do; okay?" John asked and stated at the same time.

"I never said a word to you," I grinned.

We talked for a few more minutes and I got out of John's car. Just as I closed the door John thought of another question he had for me. He hit the automatic window button and lowered the window on the passenger's side to ask me. I knelt down and peered back through the open window towards John.

"Have you heard anything from Mike Bishop? You did say he had gone down to Mexico, right?" John asked.

"That's right. I haven't heard anything recently, but I expect to hear from him any time now."

I don't know what made me glance back at the car that was slowly approaching John's car from the rear, but I did. As it drew alongside, the air was suddenly filled with gunfire. I instantly hit the sidewalk face down as I heard the gunfire and the distinct sound of bullets hitting metal and glass; and then I heard the squeal of tires as the car d sped off down the street.

Slowly I raised my head and watched the light bronze colored sedan as it raced away. As it neared the first intersection, the car's break lights flashed as the driver made the turn, disappearing around the corner. It was only then that I looked inside the car towards John.

"Are you all right...," I started to say, but didn't finish my question.

John was slumped to one side and not moving. There was blood on both the seat and the dashboard. I knew he was hurt bad and prayed he wasn't dead. I quickly felt for a pulse and found one, albeit weak. As people poured out of the businesses along the street I dialed 911 on my cell phone and then, after telling them to send the police and an ambulance, attended to my seriously wounded friend.

CHAPTER

11

I LOOKED ON in silence as the paramedics worked feverishly over my good friend, John Hernandez. John was still alive, but hanging on only by a thread. As I fielded the questions thrown at me by the police I tried to keep an eye and an ear open towards the paramedics. I heard one of them say it didn't look good and they might lose John on the way to the hospital. I prayed that God would spare my friends life.

"Can't you hurry it up, Officer? I want to follow the ambulance to the hospital. John's a good friend of mine. I grew up with him and his brother David and sister Pearl. In fact, I'd better call them right away," I said firmly.

"Just a few more questions, Mr. Castle, and we'll cut you loose here. Did you get a look at the license plate of the car the shots were fired from?" the officer asked.

"No, no, it was too far away by the time I raised up and looked in its direction. All I can tell you is that it was a pale bronze Lexus and headed off in that direction," I said pointing down the street and the casting a quick glance in the direction of the paramedics as they lifted the gurney they had John strapped on, into the back of the ambulance.

The policeman saw where my attention was and stated, "That about takes care of our questions for now. You can follow the ambulance, but stay around in case we have more questions."

"Yeah, if you have anymore I'll be at St. Francis where they're taking John. Thanks, Officer," I said gratefully.

I knew that the police would want to contact John's wife, so as I followed the ambulance to the hospital I called John's brother David and his sister Pearl. David lived in San Mateo and Pearl lived in El Cerrito.

Like I'd told the officer, we'd all grown up together attending the same schools in the town of Lindsay, a small farming town in the heart of California's San Joaquin Valley. Over the years we'd all migrated to the San Francisco Bay area where we'd made contact again.

David wasn't home, but I left a message with his wife as to where they had taken John. Pearl was home and said she'd come straight to the hospital. I hung up and called Myrna and told her to cancel any appointments I had for the rest of the day. I still wanted to check out the Wingate estate and see if little Danny was there, but it would have to wait until I found out if John was going to pull through or not.

John's wife, Linda, arrived about ten minutes after me and Pearl arrived about a half hour after I had gotten to the hospital. They had John in surgery and I expected it would be quite awhile before we learned anything. Every minute he remained alive, however, offered a measure of hope.

David Hernandez arrived about a half hour after Pearl. We talked for a few minutes and the doctor came out of surgery. He wore a very serious look on his face and to tell you the truth, I expected the worst.

"I won't pull any punches with you. He's alive, but just barely. If he can make it for twenty four hours his chances of pulling through will increase considerably. We were able to get the bullets out, but there was a lot of damage done. It's going to take a long time to recover, if he does come through this. I just wanted to tell you how it is. I'm truly sorry I don't have better news. To be honest with you...the rest is in God's hands."

Linda broke down and began to cry. I put my arm around her shoulder and tried to comfort her as best I could, as did David and Pearl. After several minutes I pulled David off to one side and told him I had to go, but please call me the minute there was any change...either way. He said he would and thanked me for being there. I gave him my business card and scribbled my cell phone number on the back of it.

The drive to the Wingate's went by fast seeing as how my mind was still back at the hospital with John Hernandez. I barely recalled what traffic was like. A lot of my trip was done in silent prayer.

When I arrived at the front gate of the Wingate's I could see three cars parked in the huge driveway in front of the house. I pushed the buzzer and waited for someone to answer. After a good fifteen seconds I hit the buzzer again. When no one answered after another fifteen seconds, I began to have a strange feeling. I've had these feelings before and they were usually right on.

Giving them one more chance and still not receiving an answer, I got out of my car and climbed over the wall near the tall gate. I walked up the driveway and hoped no one drove up to the gate with an electronic gate opener; because my car had the driveway blocked.

When I reached the front door of the house I rang the doorbell and waited for a butler or maid to answer; I waited, but no one showed. I hit the buzzer again and still no answer. My uneasy feeling was getting much more uneasy now.

I walked to the huge picture window and peered in. I could see the large entryway and a winding staircase, but there

Raymond D. Mason

was no sign of anyone. I walked around the side of the house and came to a six foot high brick wall that encompassed the entire back yard. I tried the gate latch and found it to be unlocked.

Following a neatly landscaped walkway, I made my way to the back yard of the mansion. Another gate in a four foot white picket fence that crossed from the house to the brick fence greeted me. It had no lock on it, merely a latch. I opened it and walked into the back yard.

There was a large swimming pool shaped like a figure eight or Marilyn Monroe's figure. Around poolside were a number of umbrella covered tables and chairs, all appropriately positioned to take advantage of the sun's thermal rays, but without having to contend with the sun's direct light.

It wasn't until I looked up the terraced walkway in the direction of the house that I saw the dead bodies. There were three men on the landing nearest the doublewide glass doors lying face down on the concrete   Blood spattered on the glass and concrete told me the men had all been shot, obviously with an automatic weapon. Instinctively I drew my .38 from its shoulder holster.

Shocked at the sight, I moved carefully towards the bodies to check for any signs of life. As I drew near the pool I saw the bodies of two women in the water. I noticed that each woman had two bullet slug entry wounds in the back. Just by the location of the wounds I knew the women were both dead. That and the fact that they were floating face down in the water.

A glance in the direction of the Jacuzzi turned up another woman's body. She too was dead. I froze for a moment just staring at the macabre scene I'd walked into. As I stood there surveying the bloody scene some movement off to my right caught my attention. The movement came from the direction of the cabana.

Moving quickly towards the bathhouse while keeping some of the umbrella covered tables between me and the cabana, I pressed my back against the wall next to the door. Taking a series of quick peeks inside the small building through the door that was slightly ajar, I determined that whoever was in there had gone through a back door. Either the door led outside or to another changing room.

Crouching as low as I possibly could, I moved inside the cabana. I took cover behind a large sofa that was positioned to give anyone sitting on it a good view of the pool area through the big picture window. I kept my .38 trained on the door that led to a closet, a changing room, or the back of the building, as I moved closer to it.

I stood to one side of the door just in case someone starting firing through the door. As I listened carefully I realized that whoever was on the other side of the door wasn't the one responsible for the killings. I could hear the sound of a woman crying. She was crying softly, but crying none the less.

Slowly I turned the doorknob and eased the door open. The door led to a changing room with a shower stall in one corner and a vanity on the other side of the room. There were a couple of small racks with various styles and sizes of swimwear for both men and women hanging on them. The woman was cowering in a far corner.

By the woman's uniform I could tell she was the maid. She was a black woman of about twenty five years of age and very pretty. She was also very scared. In her hand was a rat tailed comb that she was holding in a defensive position. It wouldn't have done much good against the weapons that were used on the victims outside, however.

"It's all right, young lady; I'm not going to hurt you. What happened here, anyway?" I said in as calm a voice as I could muster.

She didn't say anything at first; the fear in her eyes paralyzing her. I moved into the room very slowly and slid my pistol back into its holster. She seemed to relax slightly, but remained in her crouching position.

"What happened here?" I repeated.

This time the words seemed to make their way through her fear frozen mind and she blinked several times in rapid succession. Slowly she raised herself up to a standing position and began to shake her head back and forth, closing her eyes for a moment.

She swallowed hard and took a deep breath, "Two men started shooting. They killed them; they killed them all," she said.

"Two men; were they big men; very tall men?" I asked quietly.

She looked at me with a blank look, "They killed them all."

"Where were you?" I asked.

Again she looked at me with a distant glaze in her eyes, "Here."

"You were in the cabana, huh. They must not have known you were here," I said more to myself than to her. "Where is a telephone...?" I asked, but then noticed a phone next to the vanity before I finished the question.

"They killed them all," the woman repeated as if in a trance.

I called 911 and once I'd finished the call, led the young woman to the sofa and had her sit down. I got her a glass of water and handed it to her. She looked at it with glazed eyes for a moment, but finally took the glass. I told her I'd be right back and used the opportunity to check inside the house before the police arrived.

The first room I checked was a large, well stocked library. I noted a couple of the author's names and recognized them right away. One that fully caught my eye and attention was a book entitled, "Famous Quotes of Elizabeth Gurley Flynn and

Roger Baldwin. Right next to that book was one entitled, "Agnes Smedley, Patriot." I almost choked when I saw that title. Then I noticed the author's name; Camille Wingate. I quickly checked the author's name on the Famous Quotes book and saw it had been written by Lloyd Wingate. That told me all I needed to know about the Wingate couple. I moved from the book shelf to the huge desk in front of the large picture window. I found the center drawer was locked but was able to jimmy it open with no trouble. The drawer contained some very valuable information. I found a letter from Cory Brisbane. This had to be the same Cory that Singleton had received the call from concerning Rueben LaPorte's death. Brisbane's name didn't ring a bell; not right then, anyway.

I didn't get a chance to read the letter due to the fact that I heard the wail of the police sirens as they drew near. I slipped the letter from Brisbane into my inside coat pocket and went back outside. I'd just gotten back to the cabana when the police arrived. Now for a ton of questions, and hopefully, a few answers from the Wingate's maid in the process.

CHAPTER

12

B Y THE TIME the police had finished with their questioning of the maid and me, I was exhausted; I'm sure she was as well. All I wanted to do was go home and take a hot shower and try to wash away some of the filth I felt I was carrying around with me. Murder is such an evil act. The taking of human life is not something that normal people even want to think about. Murder is robbing someone of the most precious thing they have, their life. It was obvious though, that the people involved in this case were not normal people.

I'd managed to keep the police from finding out about the letter I'd taken from the Wingate's desk. It was only when I got back to my condo that I had a chance to read Brisbane's letter. What I read brought an ever widening smile to my face. Brisbane's letter contained some names of people that were active players in this highly profitable game of baby selling; names that were readily recognizable.

The letter explained in detail the racket that had been responsible for Norma Turner's little Danny being taken from her while she was recovering from her nervous breakdown.

The people that wanted to bypass the adoption system involved large sums of money; anywhere from ten thousand to twenty five thousand dollars.

The letter went on to say that all the parents were members of a New World Order movement known as World with No Borders. When I read that part of the letter I actually shuddered at the thought of a government like that group sought. It was an extreme form of communism unlike anything the world had ever seen. I'd heard enough about the group to know that they would stop at nothing to bring about their agenda.

The letter was addressed to Marion Beauchamp, the mayor of San Francisco, with courtesy copies to Horace Linsicomb, a lawyer with the ACLU; Mara Powell, US Congresswoman. And then a name that told me all I needed to know about the two goons that I'd had run ins with; Armand Poretti, local godfather.

I knew the Poretti family pretty well, having arrested various family members and family soldiers when I was with the SFPD. They carried the name filth to a new low. Armand had been involved in everything from prostitution to kidnapping; from murder for hire to drug running. I'd hate to have my name linked with his in any kind of transaction unless it was an arrest report and I was the arresting officer.

As for the other names, I wasn't really surprised about them either; not after considering their actions of late. Take the San Francisco mayor for instance; he had declared San Francisco a safe haven for illegals. That would most definitely include terrorists that wanted nothing more than to hatch new ways to bring death and destruction to innocent Americans. No, this guy was capable of anything due to the corruptness of his heart.

Horace Linsicomb worked as a lawyer for one of free America's worst enemies, the ACLU. He'd been instrumental in getting a convicted sex offender released from prison, only to have him go out and rape a mother and then kill her and her twelve year old daughter. When asked about the crime he blamed the pervert's neighbors for the man's behavior, saying they had printed up posters identifying the man as a sex offender and posted them in the neighborhood where the man lived. Like that had something to do with his actions; I don't think so.

The ACLU had changed their name several times through the years, since first being formed during World War I as, the American Union against Militarism. They changed their name to, The National Civil Liberties Bureau, a party whose membership included Socialist Party notable Norman Thomas; the future Communist Party chairman Elizabeth Gurley Flynn, and Soviet agent Agnes Smedley. Names I'd seen on the books in the Wingate's library.

Roger Nash Baldwin, an active member in the communist movement in the 1930's, later founded and was director of the American Civil Liberties Union. The sole purpose of the ACLU was, and is, to replace our form of government with a communistic government.

The name Mara Powell in the letter was also quite understandable. She had been an advocate of the federal government's rearing of any baby born to an unmarried teenager under the age of 18. She had tried unsuccessfully to get bills passed that would make it a federal law; fortunately her efforts had met with resounding defeat. From what I'd heard, however, she had picked up more support from some of her more radically liberal colleagues with each failed attempt.

This letter was not going to help me locate Norma's little Danny any sooner, but it gave me a head's up as to the clout of the people I might be dealing with on this case. One thing you don't want to do is bring a charge against one of these people without having a substantial amount of hard evidence to back it up. They will stop at nothing, and I do mean nothing, to attack anyone that shines the light of truth on their shady dealings. I knew I would have to tread as carefully as a man walking through a mine field. One false step and my career, not to mention my life, could be blown to smithereens. I was still staring at the letter when my phone rang.

"Hello, Nick Castle," I said grabbing up the phone.

"Buenos Dias, Mi Amigo," Michael Bishop said on the other end.

"Michael, my man; am I glad to hear from you. Have you found out anything down there?" I asked quickly.

"Have I ever Nick! I just found our Dr. Christopher Langford and guess where?"

Before I could answer Michael told me, "In the cemetery. He was murdered by an unknown assailant as he went for his morning stroll around the gated community he lived in. That is the only homicide this place has ever had. I talked to his wife and she said she didn't know why anyone would want to kill her husband; it certainly wasn't robbery. His wallet still had over two hundred dollars in it when his body was found."

"Great...well, there's another dead end...literally," I said, my disappointment apparent.

"Yeah, but listen to this, Nicky, old boy; his wife told me that just before her husband was murdered he was visited by two men asking about Danny Turner. She gave me a description of the two men and one of them sounded a lot like Ruben LaPorte."

"Well, you can drop him off your active list of suspects, Michael; LaPorte is dead. Someone made sure he would never talk to anyone, about anything, ever again."

"LaPorte is dead, huh? I can't say I'm sorry to hear that bit of news. That kind of makes you wonder about these people, doesn't it?" Michael said and then paused for a second. "Nick...you'd better watch yourself; I have a feeling we're skating on thin ice. I'll catch the next plane back."

"You watch yourself, too, Michael. Someone may be keeping an eye on Mrs. Langford. If this operation is as big as I think it is, it crosses international boundaries. I have some names of people involved in this that will make your head swim. And they're big; all the way to the top, big."

"Government big," Michael asked?

"Yep, government big; all the way to the halls of Congress," I replied.

"I'm out of here. I'll see you as soon as I can get back. Take care, old buddy," Michael said.

I hung up and looked at the letter I was still holding in my hand. This was one hot item I had in my possession. If they knew I had it my life wouldn't be worth a plug nickel. It needed to be secreted away in a safe place.

Looking around the room I spotted just the place. Removing a loosened brick I placed the letter and the envelope inside the vacant spot I had had installed when the fireplace was built. No one would ever think to look for important papers in a fireplace. I know I wouldn't.

I took a shower that I hoped would wash away some of the filth this case presented. It's hard to imagine people being so power hungry that they would stoop to some of the things they do to achieve their evil goals. As I thought about it, I realized that so much of what we do here on earth is directed by higher powers. The entire human race is involved in a spiritual battle that we see played out through our actions and/or the actions of others.

If there is a spirit of love and goodness, then there has to be a spirit of hatred and evil. Some people obey the spirit that directs them to do good towards their fellowman, and for the right reason; while others seek to do evil towards their fellowman by heading up oppressive governments. The more laws a government has the more oppressed the people become. Our government enacts somewhere around two thousand new laws each year. That's a scary thought.

CHAPTER

13

MYRNA THOMPSON poured me a cup of coffee
and eyed my face very closely.
"Are you feeling all right, Nick?" she asked.
"Yeah, why do you ask?"
"You have circles under your eyes and you look a little
pale. Are you sure you feel all right?"
"I didn't get much sleep last night, that's all. This case is
weighing so heavy on my mind I had a rough time going to
sleep and when I did, the dreams I had woke me up. This
thing is bigger than I ever anticipated it to be. And I don't
know if we're ever going to locate little Danny Turner," I said
truthfully.
"I read all about the killings at the Wingate's; that must
have been gruesome," Myra said, making a face as she spoke.
"It wasn't a pretty sight, that's for sure. I really feel for the
maid that witnessed the whole thing. She may never recover
from this ordeal. I tell you, Myrna, I've been through the
wringer. First two guys in a Lexus try to kill me and get John
Hernandez instead, and then two gunmen, maybe the same
two, murder the Wingate's and four other people. Yeah, I
must look pretty bad today."

"Let me get you another cup of coffee," Myrna said.

"Thanks, I could use another cup."

I called Linda Hernandez to see if there was any change in John's condition and she said his vital signs had improved slightly. I told her that if she needed anything to give me a call. I told her I wanted to find those responsible for this, and would if it was the last thing I ever did.   Linda didn't comment. She'd seen the results of violence too often to say anything one way or another.

When I hung up I looked at the letter I'd found at the Wingate's one more time.

"Myrna, would you get on the computer and find out all you can about a guy named Cory Brisbane. This guy's tied up in this mess as much as any one. Also, check and see what you can find out about Julian, or Julie, Rossi. Let me know what you find out on these two as soon as you turn something up," I said.

"Okay, Nick; I'll get right on it," Myrna paused. "Do you think you'll get Norma Turner's baby back for her, Nick?"

"Yeah, I think so, Myrna. Why," I asked?

"I have been thinking how torn up she must be."

"I'll be glad when Michael gets back from Mexico. There's a couple of angles I want him to start working on. He should be back sometime this afternoon," I said more to myself than to Myrna.

Within an hour Myrna had a dozen pages of print on both Julian Rossi and Cory Brisbane. Rossi was by far the more interesting of the two, although Brisbane's bio was far from being dull reading. But the information on Rossi was spellbinding.

He was definitely an insider with the Washington, D. C. crowd. There were more stories about him and senators and congressmen going on outings and vacations together than you could shake a congressman or a senator at. This guy was at every government function and always with a beautiful woman; and always a different one. But then I guess if you run a stable of call girls you can do that.

One story in particular caught my eye. There was a photograph of Rossi and Marion Beauchamp on San Francisco's Fisherman's Wharf standing by a cart load of fish. Rossi was holding up a Red Rock Cod or Sea Bass or some other kind of fish and grinning like a Cheshire cat.

I could read the name of the restaurant the cart belonged to and recognized it as a name I'd ran across a number of times. The name was Stagnaro and they were big in the commercial fishing industry. They had a fishing fleet up and down the California coast from San Diego to Crescent City.

John Stagnaro, one of the sons of Vito Stagnaro, had been busted for smuggling cocaine into Santa Cruz, California, but had beat the rap when the goods suddenly vanished from a police evidence file room. The Stagnaros and the Poretti family had been at odds for decades.

If Rossi was chummy with the Stagnaros then that meant he wasn't on the best of terms with the Poretti family. The Wingate's were Rossi's sister and brother-in-law, so the ones that killed them might be tied to the Poretti clan. I'd always had my suspicions about Marion Beauchamp, the mayor of San Francisco, and they'd just gotten stronger seeing this picture.

After I'd checked out everything Myrna had gathered together on Rossi, I went to Cory Brisbane's stack of papers. The first thing I read about him was that he was into plastics. He had a warehouse down on the wharf that had been dedicated by the mayor, several council persons, and another familiar face, Lloyd Wingate.

The warehouse was where he stored the various types of plastic ware he imported into the country from China, Korea, Thailand, and Viet Nam. The article went on to say that his business had netted him over one million dollars the first year. It also gave the address of the warehouse.

Curiosity is a crazy thing. Sometimes the most unlikely piece of evidence will stir up a lot of curiosity. Usually it amounts to nothing, but once in awhile you strike pay dirt. My curiosity was peaked in regards to the plastic products in Brisbane's warehouse.

I was just about to tell Myrna I was going to be gone for awhile when the door opened and in walked Michael Bishop. He was wearing a big sombrero and had a serape draped over his shoulder.

"Buenos Aires," he said with a big grin.

"I think you mean Buenos Dias don't you, Michael?" Myrna laughed.

"No, Buenos Aires; that's where I want to go next time I fly south," Michael grinned.

I waited for him to explain himself which followed almost immediately.

"Buenos Aires is where one of the biggest black market baby movers lives. His name is Alexis Olmos. I didn't go down there on this trip, however, because Mr. Olmos is right here in San Francisco. And you'll never guess where he's staying at," Michael grinned widely.

I waited for his answer, but Michael just stood there in his sombrero and serape and looked from me to Myrna and back again. Finally I broke the tortured silence.

"Well, where?" I asked.

"Aren't you going to guess?" Michael asked seriously.

"Okay, the San Francisco zoo," Myrna piped up.

"I'll say the Observatory," I chimed in.

"You're both wrong. He's staying as a guest with the mayor, Marion Beauchamp. What do you think about that?" Michael beamed.

"Are you sure? How'd you come up with that information when you've been in Mexico?" I wondered.

"That's where I found out about it. I was waiting in the boarding area to come back and I overheard one of the passengers, a Brazilian man, say that Alexis Olmos was flying to San Francisco. I had never heard of the man, so I asked him if he was a celebrity or something and he told me that Olmos was well known in Buenos Aires as a notorious baby broker. Of course the man said all this in a whisper. It seems that Mr. Olmos is a man you don't want to get on his bad side."

"So he's a guest of our illustrious mayor, is he? That man has more dirt on him than a grub worm. I think we'd better start doing a little dirt digging on our mayor. But first Michael, how would you like to do a little night snooping down on the waterfront? I think a little reconnoitering is in order. Are you up to it?"

"You mean breaking and entering?" Michael grinned.

"No, just entering; I don't think we'll break anything," I answered.

"Oh, shoot, I like it when we break things."

"I know a few heads I'd like to break about now, but we'll have to wait awhile."

I paused deep in thought.

"I guess this baby black market is bigger than we first thought, huh? At first I figured it was just a few doctors and their henchmen, but it looks like we've got some big hitters in this game."

I looked at Myrna and she answered before I had a chance to even ask.

"I'll get everything I can on this Olmos character, Nick. Give me an hour," she said as she got up and went to the computer.

While she busied herself getting data on Olmos I filled Michael in on everything I'd learned about those involved in the case. When I mentioned Julian Rossi, Michael did a double take.

"You know that name, Michael?"

"Yeah, I know that name really well. Julian Rossi married Vito Stagnaro's youngest daughter. They had a big wedding down in Long Beach a few years back. I'm surprised you didn't know about it, Nick. Rossi gave Sophia Stagnaro a diamond ring that would choke Moby Dick. Are you sure you don't remember it?"

"No, I don't. It must have been one that slipped by me. Hey, wait a minute. That may have been about the time that Karen Ferris and I went to British Columbia on vacation. We were gone for several weeks," I said thinking back.

"I think you're right. It was about that time."

"That explains the picture of Rossi and Beauchamp at the Stagnaro restaurant down on Fisherman's wharf," I said thinking aloud.

"What picture?" Michael asked.

"Oh, this one," I said and handed the stack of papers on Rossi to him.

Michael looked through the papers until he found the one with Rossi and Beauchamp holding up the fish. He thumbed through the other papers and suddenly stopped.

"Well, well, well; what have we here?" he said.

"What is it, did you see something interesting," I asked?

"Right here; see this? This guy next to Rossi and Senator Markey. Do you know who this guy is?" Michael asked.

I looked at the photo, "No, I don't."

"Guess," Michael said.

"Allen 'Rocky' Lane," I stated, saying the first name that popped into my head.

"No, this is none other than the man from Buenos Aires, Alex Olmos."

I couldn't believe my ears. I looked at the newspaper article under the small photo and it told of the donation to Markey's re-election campaign that Rossi had made. I figured that not only had he contributed to the senator's campaign, but so had Olmos which would be in direct violation of campaign finance laws.

This is why I hate getting involved in cases that have ties to governments, be it local, state, or federal. There is always a trail of money that leads to people of questionable reputations giving large sums of money to the candidate of their choice, thus having a strangle hold on that particular politician as long as they hold office. This is another good reason for term limits.

I could see that there were enough ties to political figures to make this case more dangerous than a pit full of vipers. My main concern was to get little Danny back for Norma Turner, but nothing would please me more than to help bring down this black market baby racket. But first things first.

CHAPTER

14

IT WAS JUST AFTER MIDNIGHT when Michael and I parked a block away from Cory Brisbane's warehouse. I had no idea what we might find inside that would help us on the Turner case. But like I said, I was curious and my curiosity had to be satisfied.

Michael had the lock picked within ten seconds and we opened the huge door just enough to slip through. There were four lights on in the huge warehouse, but no night watchman. The main security was the ones that made their routine rounds around the waterfront. Michael knew what their times were and we'd be long gone before they came around again.

There were large wooden crates marked 'Fragile', stacked three high inside the warehouse. I'd estimate a total of somewhere around one hundred of the crates were stacked throughout the place. There were five much larger containers in the middle of the other crates.

Now what plastic product would have 'fragile' marked on it? I found a crowbar on a work bench and went to work on the first small crate. There was something fragile inside the crate all right; glassware.

Michael opened another crate and found the same thing. Perhaps Brisbane had changed his import business from plastic to glassware; it could be, I thought. Then I saw Michael holding the glass up to his nose and smelling it. I knew he'd found something of importance when he smiled.

"Smell this, Nick; what does it smell like?" Michael asked.

I sniffed the glass and although it had a slightly distinct aroma to it, it didn't ring any bells with me.

"I don't know what it smells like, Michael?"

"Guess," Michael said, again with his guessing game.

"Organically grown pistachio nuts," I said quickly, not having a clue as to what the glass smelled like.

"Not even close; this is a crystallized form of meth. They blow it into glassware and when it reaches one of the super labs they melt it down and make their dope from it. Yep, that's what it is," Michael grinned widely.

"No wonder they don't have any guards on the place. Most people wouldn't even know about that," I replied.

"Yeah, and if they put a guard on the place it might stir up too much curiosity in the place. These guys know their business, that's for sure."

"Let's check the big crates," I said.

Michael grabbed the crowbar and went to work on one of the large crates. While he was doing that I moved to the office that was up a flight of stairs. There was one naked light bulb over the door which fortunately was unlocked.

I went inside the office and began to look through the desk and then the only file cabinet there. In the desk I found some bills of lading and purchase orders with 'shipped from' addresses listed as various cities in Mexico and South America filed in alphabetical order, but not much else. The bottom drawer of the file cabinet, however, was locked.

I found a metal bar near the door and used it to pop the drawer open. Inside the drawer was a metal box about the size of a 500 page paperback novel; it's dimensions being about 4.5" wide and 6.5" inches long and 2" inches thick. The box also had a tiny padlock on it, but one good whack with the metal bar is all it took to spring it open.

Inside the box were some slips of papers that had a series of numbers printed on them. The numbers seemed to be random and could mean anything. I looked at them for sometime, thumbing through the stack of papers and finding the same thing on each one; random numbers.

At the top of each paper, however, was the name of a state followed by a date. The dates on the first two papers with the name New York on top were five days apart. The date on the third paper was seven days from the paper before it. This was the pattern throughout the entire stack of papers. It still meant absolutely nothing to me. Maybe it would make sense to Michael.

I took the metal box with the papers in it with me and went down stairs to where Michael had just finished getting the top of the large crate opened. I stood on top of the crate Michael was standing on and peered inside.

There was a large printing press in this case. It was a lithograph machine that was capable of running three large rolls of paper or card stock through it at one time. The press was the size of one of my bathrooms at home. What would a guy dealing in plastic and phony glassware be doing with a lithograph machine like this?

Michael rubbed his chin as he looked at the press. He suddenly climbed down and looked at the stenciling on the side of the crate. Once he'd checked it, he moved to the next large crate.

I climbed down off the crate and asked Michael what he was looking for.

"Look at these addresses, Nick. The one we opened is heading for Seattle, this one is addressed to Chicago, this one to Philadelphia, this one to New York City, and this one over here to Miami. Do you know what these presses are used for, Nick?"

"No, what?"

"Guess," Michael said, causing me to drop my head and close my eyes.

"Printing Popeye comic books," I said quietly.

"Nope, these are presses used for printing lottery and lotto tickets. We went on a tour through one of the printing plants that prints up these tickets and they looked exactly like these. Even to the scratch off material. Did you notice the little pool like areas on the presses?"

"Yeah, I did. Are you sure about this, Michael?'

"Pretty sure. I've always said that big money invariably attracts the mob and it looks like it has done just that."

"You're right there, Michael, but it's not a crime to own these printing presses. And just because they're stored in Brisbane's warehouse doesn't mean they're going to be used to print up these tickets; although I fully expect that's what they'll be used for. Anyway, that's a matter for the police and not us. Right now I'm looking for something that will lead us to little Danny Turner."

When I said the name Danny Turner a thought hit me. I don't know why I hadn't thought of it before, but the thought lit up my brain like a Christmas tree. Danny hadn't been grabbed by someone connected to the Wingate's; no, he had been grabbed by the Poretti family!

If Rossi and the Wingate's were involved in something with the Stagnaro's then they were in the middle of a war between the two families; the Poretti family and the Stagnaro's. Little Danny was also caught in the middle of that war because he was the supposed son of the Wingate's.

The killing of the Wingate's told me that the war had heated up to a shooting war and whoever was caught in the crossfire would be fair game. We needed to locate Danny as soon as possible before he became another innocent victim in gang war. The thought sent a cold chill down my spine.

"What have you got in that metal box?" Michael asked.

"I have no idea; but it's something connected with these printing presses...I think. Let's get out of here and I'll let you take a look at this stuff when we get to the car."

We put the boards back on the crates we'd opened which didn't take long and headed for the front door of the warehouse. Just as we started to go through the small, regular sized door next to it, we heard voices outside. We both froze.

Michael put his ear to the door and listened for a second.

"It isn't security," he whispered.

Just then we heard a key being inserted into the lock. Hurriedly we took cover behind a nearby crate where we could see who was about to enter the warehouse without fear of being seen ourselves. The door opened and two men entered. One of the overhead lights gave us a good view of the men's faces. I knew both of them.

The man that had unlocked the door was none other than Theodore Singleton and the other man was Cory Brisbane. I recognized Brisbane by the photo's that Myrna had printed off the internet for me. The two of them were deep into a conversation that had worry lines etched in their foreheads.

"I'm telling you, Theo, anyone involved with the Wingate's is at risk here. The Poretti's are making hits all over the city. First it was Rueben, then they killed the Wingate's and their guests and I think we're on their hit list as well," Brisbane was saying.

"Look, Cory, I got it straight from "Chick" he's going to make sure that the old man lays off us. Armand and Vito Stagnaro have been feuding for years, but we haven't been connected with Stagnaro in any way."

"Rossi is the one that connects us to the Stagnaro family, Theo, don't you get it?"

"Well, be that as it may, Chick says that if we give the numbers to Stagnaro we're off the hook. I'd rather lose a few million dollars than my life; and after what happened to the Wingate's, I'm much more concerned about my life now," Singleton said.

The two men started for the staircase that led up to the office when all of a sudden Singleton stopped. He looked at the small crate we had opened, putting his hand on the top of it as though checking its solidity.

"What is it?" Singleton asked.

Brisbane paused, "Oh, nothing I guess. It's just one of the nails in this crate has worked its way up. I'll tap it down when we come back downstairs."

They went on up the stairs to the office. I knew that Brisbane was going for the metal box I had under my arm. I wanted to stay there and see what happened when they discovered the box was missing.

"Michael, go on back to the car and wait for me there; and slam that door as loud as you can when you exit. I want to see what they have to say about the numbers. Here, you take them with you," I whispered and handed the metal box along with my car keys to Michael.

"Okay, but be careful."

"I will, now go," I urged.

Michael moved to the doorway and stepped through. He slammed the door as hard as he could which echoed throughout the warehouse and caused me to shut my eyes from the noise. It certainly got the two old boys up in the office's attention. They scrambled down the stairs like a couple of football halfbacks running the grandstand for conditioning exercise.

"Whoever that was has the numbers," Brisbane yelled.

"My god, man, if it's Stagnaro we're dead. We'll have nothing to bargain with," Singleton said from in front of the larger Brisbane.

"We don't have anything with which to bargain no matter who it is that has the numbers. We've got to get them back," Brisbane said angrily.

The two men rushed out the door and didn't bother to close it. I could see them clearly under the outside light. They looked in both directions and when they got a glimpse of Michael started chasing after him. I saw Brisbane pull something out from under his coat. I knew what it was the moment I heard a gunshot.

I figured Michael would make it to the car well ahead of them and be able to lose them with no trouble. I just hoped he didn't forget to come back for me. I rushed to the door and peeked out.

Singleton and Brisbane were running in the direction Michael had gone, but he was no where in sight. I figured he'd already rounded the corner and must be near the car by then. I hurried out the door and ran the other way along the side of the building staying in the shadows as best I could.

When I reached the far end of the warehouse I stopped and looked back. There was no one in sight. I took a deep breath and expelled it as I turned to head in the direction of my car. The next thing I knew my head exploded into a thousand stars. Something had slammed into my head with enough force to knock me out cold.

I awoke to someone slapping my face. My hands and feet were tied to a chair and my head throbbed to beat the band. Of course, the guy slapping me didn't help the headache any. I tried to focus on the 'slapper,' but I was seeing double. Finally things started to clear up and I saw that my slapper was none other than Cory Brisbane. Standing behind him was

Theodore Singleton and next to him was a guy I'd never seen before. He must have been the one that cold cocked me.

"Come on snap out of it," Brisbane said angrily.

I shook my head just enough to lock things in.

"Yeah, yeah," I mumbled.

"Where're the numbers?" Brisbane barked.

"What numbers," I replied?

"You know what numbers I'm talking about; the ones you took from my office."

"I have no idea what you're talking about. I wasn't in your office," I lied, trying to run a bluff.

"Look, if I don't get those numbers in five seconds I'm going to turn Oscar loose on you," Brisbane threatened.

I glanced at the third man standing in front of me.

"You must be Oscar, is that right?" I said looking at the hulking figure next to Singleton.

The man grunted something that I didn't catch and stepped forward holding a blackjack. It had been a long time since I'd seen one of them, but I knew right away what it was; especially when he dangled it in front of my face.

Theodore Singleton moved up alongside Brisbane and pleaded with me to turn over the numbers.

"Look, Castle, don't make this hard on yourself. Just tell us what you did with the numbers and we'll let you go once we have them," he said looking at Brisbane for agreement.

Brisbane nodded his head yes.

"Look, gents, I'm telling you the truth. I don't have the numbers, my partner took them. I know where he was going to leave them, though," I bargained.

They looked at each other and then back at me. I could see the wheels turning in their heads as they tried to decide what to do next. I helped them out a bit.

"You give me little Danny Turner and I'll give you the numbers, how's that?"

Singleton and Brisbane's eyes locked on each other and then back at me. They both wanted to say something but neither spoke. Since they weren't going to speak I did.

"Look, I know you have the boy and you know I can get you the numbers. Now which is more important to you? I know it's not the kid."

I had the distinct feeling that these two clowns knew the whereabouts of Danny Turner. The fact that they didn't nix my offer right away told me that. I waited for their reply, and didn't have to wait long.

"We can't actually give him to you, but we can tell you where he's at," Singleton said.

"Where," I asked?

"No, no, not so fast; we haven't seen any numbers yet," Brisbane cut in.

"You'll get your numbers, you just tell me where the boy is and we'll go and get the metal box with your numbers," I said, convincing them that I had the numbers by describing the container they were in.

"Tell him, Cory," Singleton said.

Brisbane wasn't too crazy about letting me know the whereabouts of the boy before actually having the numbers in their possession. After an inner struggle with himself, however, he finally decided to give in.

"The boy is in the executive suite at the Mark Hopkins. He's there with a man named Julian Rossi. Rossi took the boy after his sister and her husband were killed," Brisbane explained.

"Okay, I'll buy that. Now if you'll untie me we can go get your numbers," I said.

They untied me and held a gun in my back as we went outside and got into a black limousine. I got in the back seat with Oscar and Singleton and Brisbane drove. Oscar reeked of garlic. I offered him a breath mint, but he didn't answer me one way or another.

There was very little conversation on the ride to my office which was good for me. It gave me time to try and come up with a plan in case Michael had not taken the box of numbers back there. It was only when I looked out the back window that I knew he hadn't; he was following us.

I spotted my car two cars back and very inconspicuous. Michael was experienced in tailing someone and I was thankful for that. My chance for getting the drop on these three had increased greatly with the addition of Michael. Now if I could just let Mike know somehow what I was going to do.

CHAPTER

15

W E PARKED across the street from the building where my office is located and got out of the car. I gave a glance in Michael's direction and saw him pull into the curb a half block behind us. He remained in the car as we started across the street.

When we reached the building entrance I noticed Michael get out of my car and start towards the front doors as well. I knew that he would catch up by the time I had signed in at the security desk which, hopefully, would help me get the drop on these three. The one I'd have to take out first would have to be Oscar. The other two shouldn't pose much of a threat.

The security guard greeted me, "Hello Mr. Castle; what brings you back here so late?"

"Just coming back to pick up a package I left in my office. How're you doing tonight, Steve?" I asked making small talk.

"Okay, not great mind you, but okay," Steve said with a chuckle, as he gave his usual response to that particular question.

After signing in the four of us walked to the elevator and took it up to my floor. As we got out and started down the hall towards my office I heard the familiar whining sound of the elevator as the doors closed and it started its descent back to the ground floor. That told me that Michael was hot on our trail.

I intentionally dropped my keys when I pulled them from my pocket in order to stall as much as I could so Michael could get closer. I knew I had to have them inside the office, however, by the time the elevator arrived back on this floor carrying my partner.

"Hurry it up, Castle; we don't have all night," Brisbane urged.

"Don't rush me...I get nervous when I'm rushed," I replied, giving him a hard look.

I opened the office door and the three of us went in. Now was the moment of truth. I searched my memory bank trying to think of anything that might look like the metal box Michael had snatched out of the warehouse office. I couldn't come up with a single thing. There was something else that I could use to buy me more time with, however; the file cabinet.

"Okay Castle, where is it," Brisbane snapped?

"Right here in this file cabinet...but, before I give it to you I want to know something. What's the room number that Rossi's in at the Mark Hopkins?"

"Quit the stalling, Castle, or I'll turn Oscar loose on you, and you don't want that, believe me," Brisbane said angrily.

"Hey, I'm putting my life on the line here and I want some kind of assurance that you're not just blowing smoke. Let me tell you something about my partner. He's the kind of guy that puts things in places in such a way that if anyone tries to open up the case containing the item in any way other than by his code, everything inside the case or container goes up in smoke. Now tell me what Rossi's room number is," I demanded

"Wait a minute; not so fast. So what you're saying is that your partner is the only one that can get to the numbers without them being destroyed?" Singleton asked anxiously.

"That's right," I said with a scowl for effect.

"Oscar, see if you can make this guy cooperate," Brisbane said, his patience coming to an end.

Oscar started moving towards me as he pulled the heavy leather wrapped sap from his coat pocket. This was going to be touch and go. I just hoped it wasn't him doing the touching with that sap and me going to slumber-land again.

The hulk was about five feet from me when the door suddenly burst open and Michael came in with gun in hand. I'd never been so happy to see him as I was right at that moment.

"Hold it right there, Hoss," Michael growled.

Oscar stopped in his tracks and turned to face Michael. Brisbane started to slide his hand under his coat, but the sound of Michael cocking the hammer back on his .38 special caused him to freeze and then slowly pull his hand away from his coat. Singleton stuck his hands in the air as high as he could reach.

"Am I glad to see you, Michael; I was running out of things to stall them with," I grinned.

"You mean you don't have the numbers?" Brisbane questioned.

"I don't; he does," I said motioning towards Michael.

"Do we still have a deal, Castle? You want the boy more than you want the numbers, and we want the numbers more than the boy; you said it earlier," Brisbane said; it was his turn to bargain now.

"Yeah, yeah, we'll make the trade. But let me tell you something. Nothing had better happen to that boy, or all bets are off. You guys are on the bad side of some very bad people so you'd better tread as lightly as if you're walking a mine field

126

while blindfolded," I warned, as I took my gun, along with the leather wrapped sap, away from Oscar.

"We'll get the boy for you," Singleton offered, a sign of resignation registering in his voice.

"What are we waiting for," I grinned.

Michael took Oscar with him in my car, having the big man drive while he held his gun on him. I had Brisbane drive the limo and Singleton sitting in the passenger's seat in the front, while I sat in the back with my gun on both of them.

When we got to the Mark Hopkins, Michael brought Oscar to the limo where he handcuffed him to the car's steering wheel. We left Oscar there while the rest of us went inside. I was glad Michael still carried a set of handcuffs with him which was something I should do also; they really come in handy at times.

Brisbane took us up to the third floor and to the room where Julian Rossi was holding the boy. Brisbane knocked on the door and waited for a response from inside. When no one answered, he knocked again and called out.

"Julian, let us in...it's Cory and Teddy."

Still there was no response from inside. Michael moved up to the door and removed a small case from his pocket. He removed a piece of metal that looked very much like a lock pick, and went to work on the lock. Within thirty seconds the door was open and we were allowed a look inside.

Julian Rossi was there all right, but there was no sign of Danny Turner. Rossi couldn't tell us anything, however, not with his throat cut the way it was. He was as dead as dead could be.

Brisbane's eyes widened to a point that I thought they might pop right out of his head; while Singleton fainted. Michael picked Singleton up off the floor and set him in a large stuffed chair and began slapping his face to wake him. I took Brisbane with me and checked out the other rooms of the massive suite.

"The Poretti's must have the boy now, Castle," Brisbane muttered.

"For your sake, Brisbane, I hope that boy is all right. We're going to have to rework our agreement. You don't have anything to bargain with anymore," I stated in no uncertain terms as we went back to where Michael had slapped Singleton awake.

"Come on, Castle; cut us some slack. It isn't our fault that the Poretti's grabbed the boy. You've got to help us," Brisbane pleaded.

"I don't have to do anything! But I'll tell you what you have to do or we'll cut you loose and let the Poretti's do to you what they did to your friend here. You're going to help us get that boy back," I said angrily meaning every word of what I said.

Brisbane wilted.

"Anything, anything you say, Castle," Brisbane agreed and cast another quick glance in Rossi's direction. "I don't want to wind up like that."

Michael and I both knew about the Poretti's and what we knew about them was all bad. Carlos Poretti had been the original godfather of the family, dating back to the thirties. He'd started out small by killing the man running a protection racket in his area of New York's, Little Italy section.

That act had endeared him to many of the local merchants until Carlos picked up where the other thug had left off. Before long he'd branched off into other areas of crime and corruption, opening up a string of brothels and Speak Easies that made him a very rich man. That's when he started buying crooked politicians.

The family business grew until they had stretched from New York to San Francisco and other countries around the world. When it came to money they had it over the Stagnaro family, hands down.

The war between the two families started when Nick Poretti tried to muscle in on some of the Stagnaro's fishing and smuggling businesses which brought about a shooting war that saw dead family members in both camps. The conflict had finally been called off by the two family heads for the simple fact it was starting to attract too much attention from the FBI.

Tony Poretti was the man that pretty much called the shots for the family in the San Francisco area and I knew Tony very well. He was a piece of work from the get go. He was a real head case with an ego that demanded constant publicity. You couldn't pick up a newspaper or a local magazine without finding a story in it somewhere that was about him or one of his favorite charities, several of which were environmental groups, something that endeared him to the city's more liberal politicians.

Nothing would make me happier than to bring this guy down with something, anything; especially something to do with Danny Turner. As long as it wasn't the boy's murder, that is. With the boy being with the Poretti's now, I had a plan that just might get little Danny back to his mama.

Everyone has at least one person that they've got a huge soft spot for, and Tony Poretti was no different from everyone else on that count. He'd been head over heels in love with one...get this, Karen Ferris, when he was younger.

When he concluded that he couldn't have her he put the word out that no one was to do anything that would make her unhappy. And that included bothering whoever she might be dating at the present or in the future. He didn't want to cause her any unhappiness in any way, shape, or form. That was the one redeeming feature about Tony; the only redeeming feature about him, I might add.

Now that Karen was back in town, she might be the catalyst that would get Danny away from the Poretti's. If I could convince her of the importance of this case, along with the fact that Poretti was punishing a woman he didn't even know by holding her little boy, she might go along with me in negotiating with Tony for little Danny's safe return.

The deal would have to be handled in the same manner as Jesus' advice to his disciples that they were to be as cunning as a serpent, but gentle as a dove. I'd play the serpent and Karen would play the dove. Now the trick was getting past her husband and getting her to go along with me on this.

Chapter
16

I CALLED THE POLICE and reported the dead body, but we were gone from the hotel long before they arrived. I didn't want to be tied up at police headquarters all night long filling out paperwork when I was this close to finding little Danny Turner.

Michael, Singleton, Brisbane, and I all went back to the limo where Oscar was waiting, still handcuffed to the steering wheel. We all got in the car and had Oscar drive us to an all night coffee shop where we went in to have a long and very informative conversation.

I had to get in touch with Karen Ferris Ciccarelli and fast. I'd seen her at Singleton's house, maybe he could tell me where she was staying. It was hard for me to bring myself to ask this guy her whereabouts, but I had to.

"Singleton, I think you know a Mrs. Karen Ferris Ciccarelli, am I right?" I asked, almost angrily.

"Karen, why, yes I know Karen; how do you know her," Singleton asked?

"Let's just say we're old friends and leave it at that, shall we," I growled.

"What ever you say, Castle; but, what do you want to know about her?"

"I want to know how I can get in touch with her," I replied.

"You do know that she's married, do you not?" Singleton asked almost as though enjoying seeing my torment.

"I know she's married; I want her to help me get little Danny Turner back from the Poretti family," I said harshly.

"How is she going to do that? Her husband is Dick Ciccarelli, did you know that?" Singleton asked seriously.

"No, I guess I didn't know that; should I be impressed by that fact?"

"Dick Ciccarelli is a very wealthy man and he got that way through his association with the Stagnaro family. I don't think he's going to be too agreeable to allow his wife to help anyone that wants to do business with the Poretti family," Singleton stated.

"What kind of business is he in, anyway?" I asked.

"He's in the import business...medicine."

The way he said 'medicine' suggested to me that Mr. Ciccarelli was in the illegal drug business. My heart ached when I thought that Karen might be married to a guy involved with the likes of the Stagnaros.

Singleton must have read the expression on my face, because he didn't waste any time hitting me with the next bit of bad news, which hit me even harder.

"He's also into...human relations and placement, if you know what I mean?" Singleton said with a kind of sick grin on his face.

I felt the skin across my forehead tighten as my anger swelled inside me.

"Quit the word games, Singleton and talk straight. Do you mean that Ciccarelli is in the baby selling racket?"

Singleton realized he had overstepped his bounds, but it was too late. He wanted to drop the subject now, but knew I wasn't about to allow that.

"I think I've said too much as it is," he said.

"I think you'd better talk more or I'm going to take this sap of Oscar's and do a number on you. Now talk and talk fast," I growled.

Singleton swallowed hard causing his Adam's apple to dance like a cork on a fishing line. As his cohort, Brisbane, stood by shaking his head negatively, Singleton told me what I wanted to know.

"You'll be sorry, Theodore; Ciccarelli is going to be very upset," Brisbane offered.

"I'm not going to take a beating for the likes of him, Cory; not on your life. I think it's time we come clean and level with Castle on everything," Singleton said looking from Brisbane to me.

"I think so, too, Singleton. My patience has just about reached its end," I encouraged.

"Okay, but leave me out of it, Theo. I want nothing to do with this; it's all on your head, remember that," Brisbane said and slapped his hands together as if wiping them clean.

Singleton talked as Michael and I listened intently.

"Danny Turner is with the Ciccarelli's right now. He's not with the Poretti family. The Wingate's originally bought the Turner boy from the Institute where Ruben LaPorte worked. I think you already know about that, right?" Singleton asked.

I nodded my head yes, "Go ahead."

"Well, Mrs. Turner somehow found out about the baby she'd had while under treatment at the Institute and somehow was able to locate his whereabouts. We figured she had kidnapped the boy, but we were in no position to go to the police about it.

"We went to the Stagnaro family with our problem and they put a couple of guys out trying to locate the boy's whereabouts. Mrs. Turner laid a good false trail by reporting him missing and then hiring you. That little ploy of hers ate up a lot of time, but the men eventually found him. The other day we grabbed him when he went out to play in the back yard of the place where he was staying.

"With the war between the Stagnaro family and the Poretti's heating up we all became very concerned. When LaPorte wound up dead, we knew that it was the Poretti's doing. And then the massacre at the Wingate's...you know about that, because you discovered their bodies and reported it to the police.

"It was only by accident that the Turner kid wasn't killed right along with the others. The truth is he was with..." he paused for a moment before continuing, "Karen Ciccarelli at the San Francisco Zoo that day. Fortunately she heard about the murders on the radio before she took him home. She brought him to my house.

"We tried to figure out what to do with the boy then, and Karen said she would take him. She loves kids, you know. I didn't really care at that point since the Wingate's were dead. They were the ones that had purchased him."

"So why did you have us go to Julian Rossi's place?" I asked, pretty much knowing the answer already.

"The Ciccarelli's were staying in the suite with him. As you noticed it has three bedrooms."

"So what are these numbers in the black box all about?" I asked bluntly.

"The numbers unlock a code to several state run lotteries. Whoever has these numbers could forge the lottery tickets of the appropriate state and assign them the winning numbers. I guess you noticed that we have the printing presses all ready in our warehouse.

"We were going to flood the market with winning numbers, but after we'd already collected the money. That way any investigation that occurred as a result would be focused on the states and not on us. The Stagnaros had it set up to point the finger of blame at the Poretti family. It looks like someone told the Poretti's before we could pull the thing off.

"The Poretti's said that if we would turn over the numbers to them, they'd let us go. We feared they'd double cross us after what happened to the Wingate's and that's why we were going to try and get you to negotiate on our behalf. We were desperate...and still are for that matter," Singleton confessed.

I took all this in as did Michael Bishop. When Singleton finished, both Michael and I asked the same question at the same time.

"Where's the boy," we asked?

"Like I said before, he must be with Karen Ciccarelli; wherever she is?"

"Something's not right here, Singleton? Where is Karen's husband, this Dick Ciccarelli?"

"I don't know, Castle honestly. Maybe they got a tip, or maybe whoever killed Rossi took them along with them; I don't know."

"Well, if the Poretti's have the boy and the Ciccarelli's, I think I know where they would take them," I said and looked at Michael.

Michael nodded in agreement with what I was thinking, "Tony Poretti's place," he said quietly.

"You've got it partner," I said. "I think we'd better do a little bargaining with the Poretti family. And since we've got what they want I think they'll do business with us."

Brisbane and Singleton looked at me and then at one another and then back at me.

"You mean you'll talk to the Poretti's?" Brisbane asked suspiciously.

"That's what I said. Give me a few minutes to make some arrangements and I'll take care of it."

"I know where Tony lives, Nick; I was there a couple of times when I was on the force," Michael said with a frown.

"We owe you for this, Castle," Brisbane said.

"Yeah, I know," I replied, which brought a smile to both men's faces.

"We'll take you back to the office so I can pick up my car and I want you two to go to the Quality Inn in Burlingame, near the airport, and register under the names of John Smith and Joe Doakes. Wait there until you hear from either Michael or me; have you got that?"

"Whatever you say, Castle; the Quality Inn near the airport." Brisbane agreed readily along with Singleton.

We left the coffee shop and went back to our office building, where Michael and I got in my car and the Three Stooges took the limo and headed for Burlingame. I knew they would do exactly as I had told them because they feared for their lives and didn't have a clue as to how to keep themselves from winding up like Rossi.

Michael and I hatched a plan that we both thought would work. We figured that Poretti had found out that Karen was back in San Francisco and had sent one or two of his goons to the hotel where her and her husband, along with Rossi, were staying. He'd ordered them not to harm either Karen or her husband, but to bring them to him. Little Danny Turner just happened to be there and the goons took him along as well.

After I'd made a phone call to the police, Michael and I headed for Tony Poretti's place in the Hillsborough hills. His house was more like a fortress than a house, however. Michael knew his way around this neighborhood because of cases he'd been involved in while on the force. I had been on the force as well, but my cases were not so much in the high rent district.

Michael stopped at the front gate of the mansion and pushed the intercom button. A voice responded that sounded more like a growl than a voice.

"Yeah, who is it and what do you want," the man growled.

"Michael Bishop and Nick Castle; we want to see Tony about some very important numbers...lottery numbers," Michael replied.

There was a slight pause, "Wait a minute," the man said.

Michael looked at me and grinned. He knew what the guy was doing, as did I. He was asking Tony if he wanted to talk to two guys about lottery ticket numbers.

"We're in," Michael said quietly.

Just then the gate swung open allowing us to enter.

"See," Michael laughed.

We drove up the long driveway to a well lit house that resembled a hotel due to its size. The landscaping was beautiful which was standard for this neighborhood. Anyone without a complete gardening crew wasn't welcomed up here.

Michael pulled in a parking space between a Lexus and a Mercedes and we got out, but not before leaving our pistols on the floorboard of the car. Michael motioned towards a long winding brick walkway that led up to the double front doors of the house. There was juniper plants spaced along the walkway with some type of low lying ornamental grass planted in between each juniper.

Before we ever reached the front door it opened and a tall man in an expensive suit stood and waited for us. As we drew near he nodded for us to follow him. There was another man just inside the doorway who patted us down to make sure we weren't carrying any weapons. Michael showed the small metal box to the man.

After nodding his acknowledgment he and the first man led us to a large door that opened into a well stocked library. Michael and I both looked around the room at all the books.

The second man stood outside the door while the first man escorted us inside the room.

"I wonder who the reader is," Michael asked, quietly.

"I doubt that it's Tony, it must be his wife," I responded.

The escort turned and looked at us. I suddenly recognized the big man. He'd been forced to retire from the Oakland Raider football team a few years earlier due to a severe knee injury. It looked like he'd gone from playing with a football to working for a sleaze ball.

"Mr. Poretti will be right down," he said unsmilingly.

"Yeah," I answered, "We'll wait."

He went to the door and waited as if keeping an eye on us so we didn't try and steal any of the knickknacks or books in the room. We were joined shortly by Tony Poretti.

"Well, well, look what the cat dragged in; a couple of ex-cops," he said arrogantly.

"Yeah, but ex-cops with something you want, Tony," I replied.

"Let's see, now what would that be...stale doughnuts, maybe?" he laughed.

"No, I'd say fresh lottery ticket numbers. Are you interested in doing business or do you want to make lame jokes?" I said sternly.

His smile dropped from his face. It was time for business now.

"How'd you get the numbers?" he asked.

"Never mind that, just suffice it to say that we have them. Now, you have something we want."

"Yeah, and what might that be...some long green, I take it?"

"Nope, we may be retired from the force, but we still don't do business with the likes of you. You have a little boy that we want...Danny Turner."

Poretti looked perplexed.

"The kid, Castle; I figured you'd come for Karen. You mean you don't want her?"

"If she's in danger I'd like to take her with me. If she isn't though, I see no need for me to rescue her from you," I said seriously.

"You know she isn't in any danger from me, Castle. I wouldn't let anything happen to her. As for the kid, what's he to you?" Tony asked.

"I know his mother and she wants her son back, that's all."

"Hey, you can have the kid, but only if you have the numbers I want."

"I've got them all right. Show him the box, Michael."

Michael pulled the small black box out from under his coat where he'd been keeping it in his inside coat pocket.

Poretti grinned, "What's to keep me from just taking the numbers and not giving you the kid?"

He was just the kind of guy that would say something like that. I was hoping he would, though.

"Because if you open this little box wrong, those numbers go up in smoke," I grinned.

Tony frowned, "I figured you'd do something like that, Castle. Just a minute," he said.

He walked to the door and said something to the ex-jock who nodded and headed towards a long winding staircase. I cast a quick glance at Michael who was keeping a close eye on Poretti.

The big man was back within a minute or so and was carrying a sleepy little boy. As soon as I got a look at the boy's face I knew it was Danny Turner. Poretti held up his hand and stopped his man at the library door.

"You can see we have the boy and he's in good health. Now, let's have the numbers," Poretti said seriously.

"Tony, I know you and I know that if I give you the numbers and the instructions on how to open the case without torching the contents inside, we won't make it out of here alive. We'll leave the box with the numbers in it with you, but the directions of how to open the box without setting off the incendiary device inside we'll leave at the front gate. We don't have any use for the numbers so you don't have to worry about us trying any funny stuff," I said with an air of self assuredness.

Poretti considered what I'd said for a few seconds and nodded his head slowly.

"Okay, Castle, it's a deal. Besides, if you double cross me I know where you and Bishop live; oh, and also your secretary, Myrna Thompson," he said, and then paused. "I make it a point to know certain things about certain people."

"We're not going to double cross you," I repeated.

"There's the door, just leave the box with the numbers in it on the desk there," Poretti said with a wave of his hand.

Michael laid the box on the desk and we walked to the library entrance. I took the Turner boy from the big body guard and looked towards Poretti. I didn't say anything, but did give him a friendly nod.

I had hoped that the phone call I had made would start to come to fruition, but so far it hadn't; at least I didn't think it had at the time. We walked to the front door of the Poretti mansion and started to exit when we heard the sirens coming up from the front gate. It was the police as well as the FBI.

Eight cars came streaming into the large parking area. Michael and I stopped on the top step of the walkway and waited as two dozen men in uniforms as well as plain clothes came rushing up the brick walkway towards us.

"Castle, is this the Turner boy," Lt. Ray Salcedo asked as he rushed up to us?

"Yeah, this is him, Ray. He's all right, he's just asleep," I said as Danny opened his eyes at all the noise and commotion.

"Poretti had him?" Ray asked as the other officers and agents rushed past us and into the house.

"Yeah, he did. We just picked him up from Poretti. You'll also find a box of numbers that are part of a lottery scam they were going to pull. We found a warehouse with five lithograph machines for running off phony lottery tickets and around a hundred crates of crystallized meth in crates down on the waterfront. Brisbane and Singleton will tell you all about them. Speaking of them, did you send someone to the Quality Inn near the airport?" I asked.

"Yep, sure did; we just got a call that they were there just like you said they'd be. Who else is in the house here that we might be interested in?"

"Do you have anything on a Dick Ciccarelli?" I asked.

"Ciccarelli, are you kidding? We've got a truck load of stuff that we want to question him about...you mean he's in there?"

"That's what I heard. His wife is with him, but I doubt you have any use for her...am I right?" I asked hopefully.

"No, we don't have anything on Mrs. Ciccarelli. What were they doing here?"

"I think they were being held against their will. They'll fill you in on that though," I said and paused. "How is John Hernandez doing, have you heard?" I asked changing the subject for a moment.

"John is fine; he's going to make a full recovery, from what the doctors say. Listen, why don't you and Michael take the boy and get lost. You can come in later today and answer all the questions that the FBI boys will have for you. I'm anxious to hear the details about this case as well," Ray offered.

"Thanks, Ray; we'll see you this afternoon," I said looking at my watch.

We didn't waste any time getting away from the Poretti estate. Michael and I drove to Norma Turners where we witnessed a tearful reunion of a mother and her son. The tears were more on Norma's side than they were on Danny's though.

The little tyke had been through quite an ordeal and to be honest, he didn't really know for sure which woman was his mother. It wouldn't take too long, however, before he would know beyond a shadow of a doubt that Norma was his true mama.

Once we'd returned Danny, Michael and I drove back to the office where he'd left his car. We said goodnight and Michael headed home. I was dog tired, but I felt good. Everything had worked out better than I'd hoped. At first I thought about going up to the office, but thought better of it, going home instead.

I had just opened the door to my condominium when the phone rang. Checking my watch I thought to myself, that this had better not be a telemarketer at this time of the morning. It wasn't. It was Karen Ciccarelli.

"Hello Nick," the familiar voice said softly.

I paused for a moment, "Karen...is that you?"

"Yes. I want to thank you for what you did tonight. Ray Salcedo told me...thanks."

"Hey, think nothing of it."

"I was wondering," she paused, "do you think we might get together later and have coffee or lunch?"

"Yeah, that would be nice. Give me a number where you can be reached and I'll give you a call."

"I think it would be better if I call you. Have you changed your phone numbers since we stopped seeing each other?" Karen asked.

"No, I haven't. You'll probably have the best chance of reaching me at the office."

"Okay, Nick. I'll call you there this afternoon."

I started to say something else, something clever, but never got the chance before I heard the phone click on the other end.

Hanging up the phone I thought about everything that had happened and wondered if I really did want to see Karen again. What we'd shared at one time was gone now and old romances are like yesterday's beer; stale and flat.

Finally I decided that talking to Karen one more time wouldn't hurt. We'd talk a little about the past while we ate and then we'd say goodbye again, probably for the last time.

I went to bed that night, or should I say morning, and slept until almost ten o'clock. When I woke up I actually felt rested. The end of a successful case is the most satisfying feeling an investigator can experience. That's what keeps us in the business. It sure isn't the money, because this case didn't have much. Michael and I absorbed the expenses for his trip to Mexico and I told Norma to keep the reward money to help her and Danny get their lives going again. That's not to say that Michael and I didn't wind up with something, however.

The next morning when I started to take the suit coat I had been wearing the night before to the cleaners, I felt something in the coat pocket and pulled it out to see what it might be. It was Theodore Singleton's large wallet. It was stuffed with fifty two, one hundred dollar bills. Without any guilt, whatsoever, I pulled the bills out of his wallet and slipped them into my own. I deposited his wallet into the first mailbox I came to and went on to the office.

As I drove to the office I ran the particulars of the case through my mind. The black market baby selling industry had been dealt a minor blow by the arrest of a few small fish. The real brains and money behind it hadn't been touched, not yet anyway. They'd have to curtail their activities, however, until the air had cleared a bit from the busts made by the police and FBI.

I knew there were some big names in local and probably even state and national politics involved in this dirty business of black market baby selling. Hopefully a full investigation by the FBI would expose a few of them. The drug cartels have bought so many crooked politicians that there will always be a steady supply of illegal drugs coming into our country. The politicians rant and rave about the problem, but very little is ever done.

Norma Turner had hired me to find her little boy; and with the help of Michael and Myrna, had accomplished just that. Our efforts in finding little Danny had exposed a filthy business run by evil minded people that would do anything if the price was right; even impregnate and then steal a mother's baby, all for 'filthy lucre'.

All in all I felt very satisfied about the entire case. Fighting crime is a full time job that only gets harder with each passing year, due mainly to the decay of morals in our society. The more we force God out of our way of life, the more influence we allow His adversary to have over us.

We have banned God from our schools and they have become 'killing fields.' We have taught our young that they evolved from apes and then are shocked when they act like animals. Without a higher power to answer to, we will continue to evolve in a downward spiral. When will it all end...who knows? Who knows, but the God we have turned our backs on.

I arrived at the office before Myrna and Michael so I fixed a pot of coffee. Hopefully I'd make a halfway decent pot this time. Going into my private office, I pulled the file on Danny Turner and took out my stamp and stamp pad from the desk. It gave me great pleasure to stamp the file folder in big red letters; Case Closed.

The End

14424300R00084

Made in the USA
San Bernardino, CA
26 August 2014